A ROSE MCLAREN
MYSTERY

MURDER ON MORRISON

LIZA MILES

Dedication

To the memory of my mother
who ignited my lifelong addiction
to reading crime fiction.

Bunty Miles
May 1928 to September 2015

Acknowledgements

The writer would like to sincerely thank the following people for their professional work, support and encouragement helping prepare this novel for publication.

Mrs Ann Murray Chatterton

Mary Turner Thomson

The Novel Poolers (Bridge of Allan)

Ian Maxtone, The Write Angle

Chapter One

August 27th

Rose had usually left the shop by now. It was 8pm. She was excited by the new autumn recipes and looked forward to hearing Trixie, her apprentice, input about the toppings and decoration in the morning. Rose saw the flashing lights pull up outside and presumed it was another incident in the pub two doors away. There had been nothing but trouble there recently since the new owners had taken over. Everyone was complaining about it, it was bad for business and the local community.

Rose switched off the light and pulled open the door, but the familiar routine was brought abruptly to a halt as Sally's body fell back through the door and her head hit the *Welcome* mat at Rose's feet. The lifeless scrap of a body was barely dressed for the wet evening, a skimpy top and torn jeans were all that covered her. A needle was hanging out of her arm. It was instantly clear she was dead.

Rose stood for a moment, frozen to the spot, her hand still holding the door handle. Her eyes locked onto the

Sally's lifeless corpse. In a flash she was transported back to another doorway, another night from her own past. She had come so far since then, fought her way through so much to get where she was now. Her mind pulled itself back to Sally. Poor Sally.

The ambulance crew was yelling at her to step back.

Morrison was always busy and when Rose looked up, she saw a small crowd of onlookers had gathered, some were taking pictures, others were casually pointing and discussing what they saw, as if Sally weren't human. It was all too familiar, Rose had been there herself once, at the receiving end of the sneers, the jibes, the dehumanising comments.

Rose felt sick. The panic rose up inside and she stumbled back into the chair next to the shop window. The room was spinning, and time seemed to stand still. When she looked up she was surprised to find a uniformed female police-officer staring down at her. She had not heard anyone come in.

"Are you alright, what's your name?"

"Rose, Rose McLaren."

"Do you work here?"

"No, well yes, I own the business, this is my shop."

"I see. Do you know who that was, the woman in your doorway, do you recognise her?"

Rose swallowed, the officer's questions were matter of fact, without emotion or feeling. Rose knew the woman was just doing her job, but why couldn't she do it with more compassion?

"I know her … knew her, yes. She worked here once, her name is Sally. Do we have to do this now? I'm really shaken up."

Rose knew she was being assessed - whether she had any involvement or not in what had happened. That too was all too familiar.

"Of course, I can have someone drive you home, we can meet again tomorrow for your statement."

"Thank you."

Rose clung to the table for support as she got up, she looked through the window, the ambulance and the body were gone and most of the crowd had dispersed. She narrowed her eyes as she saw a familiar figure walking across the road, he was waving at another man, they met and fell into an embrace. It was Rob, an old friend, he had also known Sally. Rose frowned. She couldn't face breaking the news to him or to Trixie that their friend, Sally, was dead.

Chapter Two

Rose bagged up the last two ginger, honey and lemon muffins. It was just past 2pm and the sun was already on its way down. October in Edinburgh had been dreich and colder than usual. The late afternoon-tea crowd would be disappointed the new muffins were sold out, but Rose knew she didn't have time to make a fresh batch now. The ginger and lemon recipe had worked out well and there had been more demand for it than she had anticipated. Usually, a new seasonal recipe took a few days for word of mouth to get around, but this time it had taken less than a day.

"Cheers Tony, enjoy. Say hi to Babs for me," Rose said to the stylish bespectacled man in a grey suit, as he carefully placed his order into a hand-woven shopping basket, already filled with vegetables from the organic farm shop. "How is Babs?"

"Oh, not so rosy, Rose. Sorry, I didn't mean …"

"It's alright Tony. Look, so long as she has an appetite and you are there to care for her, it will all work out, I'm sure of it."

Tony allowed himself a brief smile, but it didn't reach his eyes. They both knew the outlook for his wife wasn't promising. "Well these will cheer her up, ginger is one of her favourites, and the way you've decorated them, they are a work of art."

"Not bad for a cyclops," said Rose pulling a face and pointing to her one good eye. "See you in the week, just give me a call if you need help or a delivery."

"Bye Rose and thank you."

Tony was one of the regular customers who mostly lived or worked locally around Haymarket where Rose had built her business. Muffins on Morrison had slowly and steadily grown to be a favourite with residents, workers, students and families. November 1st would be the third anniversary since she had opened, starting with half a dozen seasonally flavoured Christmas muffins and boxes of melt-in-the-mouth shortbread. The pale green and pink store with black and white pictures of glamorous stars and pin-up girls was in stark contrast to Rose's own appearance.

At five feet seven, with short dark hair, a straight back and a muscular frame, Rose was aware that her presence, to some, could be intimidating. Indeed, before she opened the shop, creating that physical presence was essential for her survival. Decorating the shop overtly fem was, in one way, a pushback to her father's final letter that the store was just another pipe dream, "more rose-tinted glasses," he had written. But in another way the decor represented the soft old-fashioned underbelly of Rose's personality. The pink and green paintwork and art deco style interior had started as a whimsical joke between her and her friend, Marion, but Rose's customers seemed to love it. Later, when she had taken a poll to find out what they thought about her plans for redecorating the doll house size shop, the result was clear. Don't change a thing.

"Do you want to take a break Trixie, I can manage, it's usually quiet now." Rose fixed her good eye on Trixie, who had started her apprenticeship earlier that summer. She was a pert red-haired trainee who looked, on the outside, more suited to fashion retail than baking muffins But Trixie's outer appearance, like Rose's, hid a deeper and more complex story.

"Ay, ta. I wish I'd put one of the new muffins by. Quite a success, ye must be pleased." Her Scottish brogue was bright and cheerful, despite the busy morning and early start.

"I am, and so should you be, that stem ginger topping was the perfect finish. Well done. Here take one of these." Rose handed her one of the breakfast muffins.

"Will ye be giving me a guid wee report then?"

"Don't push it Trixie. I still got to keep an eye on you, girl."

"Haha, I ken that. But it doesnae hurt tae ask how yer one guid eye finds me?"

Rose shook her head. Her now permanent loss of sight in one eye had become a standing joke between them, the teasing was well meant. And she preferred it to sympathy or platitudes. Rose had no room for self-pity after what she'd been through and she demanded the same of others when she tried to help them find their feet again. The macular degeneration that was diagnosed when she was twenty-three had finished her career in the RAF, she never thought she would be able to stand on her own two feet again. But she had. Sometimes juggling the role of mentor and manager took its toll and her own gremlins roared, making her snap when she knew she had been too soft, too generous, too understanding.

"Well Miss Trixie, carry on like you're doing and it will be one of the best references I could write, but screw up like the other day and …" referring to the batches of dough Trixie had burned, Rose pointed her finger to her throat and made a mock cut. Rose was smiling, but she was serious and Trixie knew it.

Trixie leaned against the shop window and took a bite from the breakfast muffin. She had never met anybody like Rose before. In fact she doubted there was another quite like her. Aye, she was hard, but fair, kind, but firm. And every time Trixie thought she had Rose figured out, she learned something new. Like the fact that she had spent three years in prison. Not that Rose had telt her, Rose didn't even know Trixie knew and she had better keep it that way. Trust that low-life, drug dealer Rob tae blab, but then why did Rose put up with him? There were other ways to get what she needed. Standing outside the store Trixie looked back at Rose cleaning the counters and rearranging what was left of the baking for sale. The sudden sound of the sirens made her jump.

Trixie turned to look across the street. A police car, a van and an ambulance had pulled up outside the student accommodation opposite as a group of young women rushed out, through the revolving door. They all seemed to be crying. A police officer went over to them while her colleagues ran into the building. Trixie was transfixed on the bustle and activity. A crowd gathered, some were holding cell phones, recording and taking photographs.

"What's going on?" said Rose, appearing through the door. "I heard sirens."

Trixie shrugged, "Looks like someone is …" her voice trailed off as she saw the paramedic return to the ambulance and take a large black object from the back.

"Dead," said Rose," that's a body bag going in. I'm sure of it."

Trixie put her hand to her mouth.

"Come on, let's go back inside. I don't want to be a looky loo at someone else's misfortune." Rose felt her stomach churn. The police van, the ambulance, all those bystanders with phones taking pictures and filming. Sally's death two months ago had brought it all back, dredging up a time in her past she would rather forget. She had been out of her head that day, yet the memory of their faces staring at her as if she was subhuman was etched in her brain. Rose shuddered as the bell on the door of the shop rang when she pushed it open. She knew just how easy it was to fall from grace, that everything she had built up could be wiped out in a heartbeat.

"Are ye awright?" asked Trixie, as she noticed Rose shudder.

"Yeah, I'm fine. Let's close up for half an hour. I could do with a break too. Tea?" But as she boiled the kettle and made two large mugs of the fresh dark liquid she knew it wasn't just tea she was really needing. Rose texted Rob.

I can't do it. Can you help?

The reply pinged in immediately.

How much?

£25.

Lightweight. Sure. After you close?

Yeah, thanks.

Rose's business did well from whatever tragedy had befallen someone at the student building. A steady stream of customers, police, reporters and students bought pretty much everything Rose had left for sale that day.

"There will be nae *days-olds* for the morrow," said Trixie as they finally cleared away and closed up. It was gone five by the time Trixie changed the notice on the door to 'closed'. Someone was tapping on the window. Trixie looked up, it was Rob.

"Och nae him Rose. He's a devil if ever there was one."

"It's okay Trixie, I said I'd put some of the leftovers to one side for him. He's not that bad." Rose's face flushed as she spoke, there were no leftovers and she hadn't learned to lie well.

"He's nae been about for a bit, thought maybe he'd been arrested, or crawled back into the shite hole he came frae."

"Wow, you really don't like him, do you?"

"And ye ken well why. I still think he was responsible for wha happened tae Sally. He's a bad yin Rose. Dinnea get mixed up wi him."

Rose sighed. She knew Rob standing there was bad for Trixie, the way the events of the afternoon had been for her. Trixie was in recovery and Rob had been one of her dealers. Why had he come so early? "It's ok, Trixie, off you go."

Trixie shrugged. She didn't want to be rude to her boss, and it was unlike her to hold her tongue, but she couldn't afford to screw up and lose the opportunity Rose was giving her. "Night then, see ye the morrow."

Rose watched Trixie walk past the police vehicles and yellow tape that were blocking most of the pavement opposite, her shoulders hunched, she had avoided making eye contact with Rob and pulled up the hood of her black jacket. Rose beckoned Rob into the shop.

There were still several onlookers hanging around outside the university accommodation as the police came and went. Rose recognised Some of them as students who regularly came into the shop.

Who had died she wondered? Hoping it wasn't a student. But her hopes were soon dashed as the five thirty local news broke the story. A male student, a foreign national, had hung himself.

Rob looked at the radio as the announcement was made. He frowned.

"You know him?"

Rob shook his head. But his face was pale.

Rose wondered if Rob thought it might be one of his customers. A second death of a buyer close to home was the last thing Rob needed. After her former apprentice Sally had died she had been vilified by the press as a rotten mother, who had put drugs before her baby, but Rose knew the other side of the story. Her addiction had been fuelled by what she had survived as a child.

Rob, as a local dealer, had come under police scrutiny then. But they hadn't really bothered. After all, Sally was hardly a priority in their eyes, just another junkie who had overdosed.

Rose paced her flat, looked at the foil wrapped parcel she had bought from Rob and cursed herself. It was almost two months since her last panic attack, the night she found Sally's body, but today's events had unsettled her equilibrium and the techniques her counsellor had shown her didn't seem to be working. Or was it her, she wondered, not getting it right, not doing them properly. Screwing up as usual. Her father's words rang through her head.

There had been no compassion when she told her father why she had to quit her childhood dream and leave the RAF. Despite the fact she was now thirty five, and the excuse of youth and insecurity no longer applied, she couldn't shake off the feeling of abandonment. The last time he had spoken to her was at her mother's funeral. Kind, beautiful, sensitive Jeannie, the love of his life.

Rose had always known that her father wanted a boy, someone to go fishing with, mend things with, go hiking with and Rose had tried hard to keep up. Her father had never understood her fascination with space, flying and the galaxies she believed were out there, ready for exploration. She had joined the Cadets hoping to please him, but it hadn't worked. His prejudices about the upper classes and the over-educated blinded him to the opportunities that Cadets offered girls like Rose. It was almost a matter of pride to him that he had apprenticed, not gone to college. To be fair he was good at what he did. He could mend anything with an engine and he had made a success of his garage. It was a business he would like to have handed on, and as he didn't have a son, a daughter would have to do. So when Rose worked hard to make sure she had the A levels to qualify as a trainee in the RAF, it had been Jeannie, her mother, who had argued with him, defended and supported Rose's ambitions, not to apprentice with her father and take over the business.

Then, just as she was about to really take off, apply for the NASA secondment programme, she failed the sight test and that was it. Her brain burst somewhere between her diagnosis, breaking up with her boyfriend of the time, Troy, and her mother's accident, a stupid fall.

One had nothing to do with the other but in Rose's father's mind, Rose was responsible for her mother's death, despite the fact that Rose was over 100 miles away. Jeannie had fallen downstairs, hit her head and died. According to the coroner, her death would have been almost instant, she would not have suffered. But his verdict brought no comfort to either Rose or her father. Rose was about to unwrap the tiny package when her phone rang. It was Rob.

"Have you heard, seen the news update?"

"Hi Rob, I'm sorry, no I've had everything switched off here, I've been stewing in memories. Not helpful."

"Hasn't the gear helped?"

"No, I'm trying to resist. I'm scared where it will take me."

"Rose, harm reduction right? You need what you need. I won't see you fall, you've come too far."

"Someone should have told Sally that, Rob, she'd been nine months' clean, and now she's dead."

"Yeah but she … Look, Sally was different, she had her monkeys and they wouldn't shut up."

"And I have gremlins, I thought they were gone, but they came back today, when I saw the police and the crowds taking photographs, that body bag. I shouldn't have sent you that text, but that's how pathetic I am."

"Sorry. Rose, I don't want to fall out with you and if you'd rather I said no when you contact me, just say that. I'm not one of the bad guys, whatever Trixie thinks. God the look she gave me through the window when I knocked."

"An honest drug dealer." Rose laughed. "Now there's a turn up. Someone should write a book about that."

"There's more to me Rose, you know that."

"Yeah Rob, I know that. Sorry, you said there was more news about the student, that's why you called."

Rob took a deep breath. "Yes, they've released his name, it was Bakti. Rose, I don't know what to do."

She waited while he gathered himself. Her voice was gentle. "I'm so sorry, I know you really liked him."

"Yeah, I thought we were getting somewhere. His family didn't know he was gay, it was bothering him because his Dad was coming to visit. Maybe that's why he did it, but I can't believe that, not really. I'm really shaken up, Rose. That's why I called you, but you've obviously got a lot on your mind, you don't need me asking you for help."

"Rob, actually, helping you will help me. Why don't you bob over? I've got things I can make a chickpea curry with. You can tell me all about Bakti."

But it wasn't Rob who arrived at Rose's door almost an hour later, just as the aromatic spices from the curry began to permeate beyond the front door of the tiny flat. It was a soaking wet Sergeant Gibson, who wanted to confirm an alibi given by a Mr Robert Kennedy for 2pm earlier that afternoon.

Rose brushed her arm and looked down. Why on earth had Rob given her as an alibi? She remembered texting him, but that was later and he could have been anywhere. He certainly wasn't in the shop at 2pm when Tony was buying the last of the ginger muffins.

"Come in, you're soaking," said Rose, biding for time as she considered how to answer the question without lying.

The policeman nodded. "Smells good, are you waiting for a guest? He inclined his head towards the small table set for two in the middle of the room.

"Yeah, actually I'm waiting for Rob, Rob Kennedy, he was coming over. Sorry, I'm very confused. Where is he now?"

"I can't say too much, but we need to know whether he was where he said he was at 2pm today, if you could confirm that, I'll be on my way. Is he a good friend of yours, boyfriend?"

Rose looked down, if she lied about seeing Rob at 2pm and they found out she would be in trouble, and if she told the truth, what would that mean for Rob?

"Definitely not a boyfriend" she replied.

She knew it would be no use asking why they were questioning him about where he was. A drug deal gone wrong? Her gut told her she needed to put distance between her and Rob as far as the police were concerned, but she didn't want to drop him in it either. She knew only too well how so-called evidence could be misread. "You know the shop was pretty busy today, I can't remember, I'm really sorry."

The policeman looked at her with a steady gaze. She could feel herself flushing with the lie. Damn Rob.

"Well, if you do remember, please get in touch. This is the number and who you should speak to." He handed her a card with the name and phone number of a Detective Inspector Chatterton.

"I will," she said nodding, hoping her vagueness had been enough for them not to need to ask her anything else about the afternoon.

The policeman looked across at the dresser where the silver foil package still sat. Rose felt her stomach plunge. Was it obvious what was inside it? Had he seen it? The lighting was low, so there was a chance he hadn't.

"'Night then Miss, I hope you enjoy your curry."

"Thanks, goodnight."

Rose leaned against the door as she closed it behind him and sighed. What the hell was Rob thinking, but at least one good thing had come out of it, she was on top of her anxiety. She wouldn't need the silver foil package after all. Rose hesitated as she considered putting it in a drawer or unwrapping the hash and flushing it. Her phone rang, she hesitated, the call was from a private number.

"Hello, Rose speaking."

It was Rob. "What did you tell them?"

"Rob, where are you?"

"I'm down the nick, you are my phone call."

"Me! Why didn't you call a, I don't know, a solicitor?"

"That's rich, I'll get a duty, don't need to phone for that. But what did you say?"

"That I couldn't remember, why did you say you were at the shop? Why are you with the police for God's sake?"

"They think I killed Bakti."

Rose froze, that couldn't be right. Why on earth would Rob kill his lover? "Rob, I can't lie, say you were in the shop at 2, Tony was there and Trixie, and Mrs thingumybob from the barre place. I looked at the clock, it was 2pm for sure because Tony just bought the last of my new ginger muffins. Where were you? If you had nothing to do with this, just tell them."

"Forget it." The line went dead.

Rose stared at her phone, willing him to ring back. But the powers of telepathy were absent, and her phone remained still and silent. Rose sat down staring out of the window. Her flat overlooked Murieston Park, the road outside was quiet and there were no runners or the usual late evening dog walkers to be seen. It was as if the world had taken an in-breath with her, everything was still, waiting for her to breathe out, release the tension that had built up once again, exposing the fragility of her recovery. She grabbed the foil package and tore off a tiny piece of the hash. She moaned as her mouth opened, an unwilling recipient of the morsel that would either help or condemn her. If only she knew which.

When the alarm pinged on her phone, almost six hours later, it was still dark. Rose was confused, she had slept on the couch and was still dressed. Her head felt woozy and as she put her feet on the floor she heard the clink of a can against the bottle.

"Idiot," she told her face as she stared into the bathroom mirror. Rose had broken not only abstinence from pot but nearly seven years of sobriety.

Trixie was leaning against the shop doorway as Rose rushed along the street. She had just had enough time to make the early recovery meeting, but she had stayed silent. Too ashamed to reveal her relapse and haunted by the prospect of a session with her sponsor by telephone later.

"You look rough," said Trixie unhelpfully as Rose unlocked the door to let them both through and start prepping for the breakfast crowd. She would normally have been here by now, six dozen muffins should already be cooling waiting for Trixie to finish them and set them up in the display cabinet.

"Stupid alarm, my battery died. We'll have to work together, fast as we can." Rose began pouring batter into the muffin cups, but her hands were shaky and she overfilled some of the cups, and splattered the batter, she clenched her jaw. "There's going to be no time for these to cool properly."

"What if we just used the sugar and nut toppings instead of the icing on those, that way cooling doesn't matter?" Trixie said calmly. She rarely saw Rose agitated like this.

"Sure, let's just get them done." Rose turned on the radio, she needed music to distract her, but it was already seven thirty and the announcer began reading the local news.

"The student, a foreign national found dead in the halls of residence on Morrison Street yesterday afternoon is now believed to have been murdered. A local man is helping the police with their inquiries."

Rose dropped the spatula. So it was true, Bakti had been murdered and Rob was helping the police. What she had hoped was a dream or the result of a bad trip and alcohol was the reality she had tried to escape from. Rob was still at the police station.

"What's the matter Rose?"

"It's Rob, the police are questioning him."

"I knew it," Trixie exclaimed. "And Sally tae, he has tae have been responsible."

"Whoa Trixie, what on earth are you talking about? How can you link Rob, Sally and this student's death together?"

"Because Rob knew both of them. He was their dealer, for goodness sake. I saw him with Bakti."

"You knew him?"

"Aye, he came tae the music meet-up's then, one night, he turned up wi' Rob, that's why I stopped going." Trixie saw the colour drain from Rose's face. "What, what is it?"

"He wanted me to give him an alibi for yesterday afternoon."

"Gotcha!" yelped Trixie, smiling. "I hope he gets put awa' forever."

"Trixie, Stop! I don't see Rob murdering anyone, especially not the boy he was starting a relationship with. And Sally, why on earth would he have killed her?"

"Ye cannae deny that the police did speak tae him aboot Sally, after she was found dead."

"Yeah, but that was about drugs and it turns out she had stopped using Rob, months before she died."

"Why are ye defending him, Rose? What's he got oan ye?"

"I'm not. Nothing. I just …. ." Rose shrugged her shoulders. "We need to get these muffins done. I don't want to talk about it anymore. Not right now anyway."

Trixie opened her mouth to speak but changed her mind. Rose was right, if they didn't get on there would be nothing in the shop when it opened at 8.30am.

The shop was busy all morning, the late start meant Rose was continually baking to catch up and making sure they had enough to sell. But her mind was elsewhere as she made up the different batters, chopped fruit and fillings. If Rob was a suspect and he had tried to use her as a false alibi, how long would it be before the police looked into her past, found out she had also spent three years in prison? How many times would her past continue to confront her, haunt her? Why had she had to contact Rob yesterday, of all days? If they checked his phone they would see her text.

But the police didn't follow up with Rose. Rob was released, then he disappeared and neither she nor Trixie mentioned him again that day. As the hours turned into days and the days turned into weeks, Rose's equilibrium returned as she prepared her shop and recipes for Christmas, until the elderly man crossing the road at the top end of Morrison Street was run over and killed. He was carrying a bag of spiced sugar plum Christmas muffins.

Chapter Three

December 23rd

Detective Inspector Chatterton took off his glasses as he listened to Rose's account about what she remembered of the elderly man. They were sitting across from each other in her tiny flat, made smaller by the large potted Christmas tree Rose had bought on impulse. This was the third time that Rose McLaren and Muffins on Morrison had turned up in an investigation in the last three months and DI Chatterton was too long in the tooth to believe in coincidence. Not that there was even the remotest chance Rose McLaren could have been directly involved in any of the deaths, but she knew something, he was sure of that. His ample gut and what was on record told him there was more to Rose McLaren than a muffin maker.

"So, no he wasn't a regular," Rose continued. "In fact I don't remember seeing him before at all. And sorry I certainly can't remember the time he came in. But obviously it was before he died."

DI Chatterton stiffened his shoulders. "This is not a joke Ms. McLaren."

"Of course not, I'm sorry, I didn't mean it the way it sounded, but surely, it was just an accident."

DI Chatterton pursed his lips. "What makes you think so?"

"I just assumed. There's been nothing on the news to suggest it was anything else."

The DI nodded. His sharp blue eyes studied Rose's face. "We don't always broadcast everything we are looking into."

"I see," said Rose. She could feel herself become unnerved, why was he telling her something that the police wanted to keep under wraps? And why had a DI come to see her, surely this was the sort of thing a constable or a more junior officer would do?

The clock on her wall struck 8pm. Rose was tired. It was two days before Christmas and she needed an early start to make sure all the additional orders would be out on time. She had had to take on a delivery person, and that meant extra wages in addition to the overtime she was paying Trixie. There was a pile of printed Excel sheets on the table next to where the DI was sitting.

"How is your business doing? Do you do everything yourself?"

It was, on the surface, an innocent enough question but Rose felt the jibe as he looked at the paperwork. Her accounts for the past year. Did he know about her history? Of course he did, how could he not know? "Oh, yes, I have to do everything myself, the profits are pretty marginal to be honest."

"I see," he said nodding sagely.

What exactly did he see, wondered Rose, was he putting two and two together and making twenty. What did he really want?

"Well, I'll leave you to your paperwork, no doubt your shop is very busy right now, with it being Christmas."

"Yes, it is. Thanks, umm," Rose paused.

He stood up, making his way to leave when she felt compelled to ask the question. Before she could stop herself the words were out. "Look why are you really here?"

The DI gave her a sardonic smile. "Why just as I said when I arrived. Is there something you have remembered, something you need to tell me?"

He was standing so close to her in the vestibule she could feel the energy from him, assessing her as if he could read her thoughts.

She could have kicked herself, why had she asked him that? Rose shook her head. "No, nothing." She brought herself up, standing tall and straight, her exterior confidence belying her creeping anxiety as she let the policeman back through the door into the hallway. She double checked the lock and slid the chain on the door.

"Breathe Rose, breathe," she told herself. She ran a bath and made a big cup of hot cocoa, she was shaking, discombobulated, drained of energy, glad that she had flushed the remainder of the foil package and poured out the rest of the bottle of vodka. Now would be the time to have a large one; she battled with the thought, determined not to relapse again.

Tony was one of the first customers the next morning. He and Babs were holding a tea party, he explained. They had decided Rose's muffins and Christmas biscuits would be centre table. "Those ginger lemons were perfect," he said, counting out some change for the tip jar Rose had put out for Trixie and the delivery driver to share between them. "Although Babs wanted to cancel after what happened."

"Sorry, what's happened?"

"Her doctor was run over, three days ago. The ambulance took him to the hospital, but he died later. Babs is so upset. He was a kind soul, almost retired."

"I knew about the accident. I didn't realise he was Bab's doctor. He'd come in for muffins, before he died. The police came to talk to me about him."

"The muffins were for Babs, she had told him about you when he last visited."

"Oh Tony, that's tragic." The image of the small balding man paying for his order, flashed in her mind along with the inspector's words from last night. "Three deaths in less than three months," and the penny as to why the DI had come to see her last night dropped. All of the deaths had a connection, albeit remotely, to Rose and her shop. Sally had been found dead outside, and Bakti and Doctor Reynolds were customers.

"Are you alright Rose?"

"Yes, sorry Tony." Rose pulled herself back into the present.

"Well at least your friend can't be accused of having anything to do with running over Dr Reynolds, his picture has been all over the place. Trial by media these days, it seems."

"My friend?"

"The one who the police questioned and who used to hang about here."

"Rob? He's not my friend Tony, just someone I know. How did you make the connection?"

"Sorry Rose, I saw him that day the student died, he was outside, when I came to get the ginger muffins."

"Outside the shop?"

"Yes."

"Tony would you mind telling the police that. I think it might be important."

"Really? Sure, I can do that. I have to call them anyway about Dr Reynolds, one or two things they're following up with. See you later."

Rose watched Tony leave the shop, there was already a queue of customers and Trixie was in the back prepping the toppings.

"Trixie, do you mind if we swap roles for a bit, can you serve?" Rose needed the space to clear her head, think about the events of the day Bakti had died and when she had texted Rob. If he was at the shop, why hadn't he come in? Why make up an alibi, when he already had one? If Tony had seen him, there would be others too.

What time had Bakti died? It couldn't have been after 2pm because she had told Trixie to take a break not long before the ambulance had arrived. Her logical mind told her there couldn't possibly be a connection to all three deaths, yet something that Trixie had said, a brown haired woman, why was that relevant, and the visit from the DI suggested otherwise. What and how she had no idea, but she had that feeling of being overrun by the same darkness from six years ago, when the police had come to Troy's office and arrested her.

Rose hadn't thought about Troy for over a year, until last night when the DI had looked at the pile of accounts on her desk. She and Troy had met almost as soon as she completed the first level of training in the RAF. He was several years older, good looking and sure of himself. Rose was very much a wallflower back then, she wasn't comfortable or confident around men, or getting dressed up. She liked being in uniform and she liked the company of women. Her figure and elfin faced androgyny made her fashionable as she was growing up, she had even once been approached by a scout for a modelling agency. Despite her reticence Rose was much admired. When Troy first saw her in the mess she was alone, and he was surrounded by a number of officers, male and female.

"Come join us." His shadow had fallen on the book she was reading as she looked up to see him standing opposite her across the table.

Rose looked over at the group. It was an unusual mix which broke the protocols and formality of age and rank.

"No, thanks, I'm about to go. I have an early start."

He leaned forward and put his hand over hers as she laid the book on the table. "So do I" he said.

His eyes dared her to refuse him and she followed him over to the group. He made sure she was included in the conversation and every time she tried to slip away he persuaded her to stay. He walked her back to her barrack, he didn't try to kiss her, but he leaned into her and asked her if she would mind if he wrote. He was being posted in two days he explained.

Rose agreed but did not expect him to follow up. He had been drinking steadily and she was sure some other girl would catch his eye. Rose didn't see him again until she was re-posted. He had written to her regularly, but she had ignored the letters. Her instincts told her he was too good looking, too popular, too sexy and she knew that to get to where she wanted to go, she would have to be disciplined, better than everybody in what she achieved. The other girls thought she was crazy.

"He's the ultimate pin-up Rose, and he wants you."

Finally she succumbed. But something hadn't felt right, she couldn't be herself around him. He distracted her from her own ambitions. He didn't take it well when Rose told him they were finished romantically. He was about to retire from the RAF and set up a business. He had big plans he told her, and she would be sorry.

.oOo.

"Rose, we need more of the ginger lemons." Trixie interrupted her thoughts "And Rob's back. He's hanging about outside of the shop."

"That's weird," said Rose.

"What dae ye mean?"

"Well Tony only just mentioned seeing him, the day Bakti died. Confirmed the alibi he gave them."

"Aye weel, whatever, he's there, large as life. We really need those gingers, like yesterday." Trixie urged, their roles reversed momentarily as Rose gathered herself and sent Rob a text.

Too busy now. Come to mine at 7pm.

"Right." Rose said. "I'm on it."

The steady stream of customers kept them both busy until closing time. The shop was finally empty and they were completely out of batters. Everything would have to be made up from scratch before tomorrow, the last day before Christmas. Rose had decided to shut at 1.30pm on Christmas Eve, to let Trixie and the delivery driver get away. Now she was regretting the decision to open at all, but they had orders to fill, and Rose didn't want to let her regulars down. She texted Rob again.

It's going to be late, so much to do. Sorry. I'm not going to be able to meet tonight.

Tomorrow? He texted back immediately. Then another. *Please.*

Rose paused. This was the season of goodwill, but her goodwill was fast running out. She had been looking forward to closing and taking a break, catching up on all the admin that she had let slip and she wanted time to go to as many meetings as she could. She knew she was on rocky ground and her sponsor had been blunt. It was way too soon after that relapse to take any risks. *OK. Late afternoon, but you have to be clean.*

Yep, promise, I just need to talk to you.

Rose pinged back a thumbs up. He was exhausting her already.

Chapter Four

December 24th and 25th

Rob was hunched over the wall outside her flat when Rose turned the corner. He was clearly not doing well.

"You'd better be clean," she muttered to herself as she closed in on him, staggering under the weight of her grocery shopping. Tony had invited her to have Christmas Day lunch with him and Babs, but Rose had refused, pleading exhaustion and the start of a cold. She had shopped to avoid the need to go out again for the whole of the five day break. Staying away from the temptation of alcohol, or passing pubs and restaurants packed with revellers making merry.

"Sorry Rose, I promise you I'm clean, and sober as a judge." Rob called out, seeing her hesitate as she approached him.

"Yeah, well make yourself useful and carry some of this up, can you?" Rose fiddled in her bag for her keys, giving herself time to check his breath inconspicuously as she handed him some of the grocery bags.

"Where are you staying?" Rose asked matter-of-factly as they unpacked the shopping together and she put on the kettle for tea.

Rob shrugged. "Can't you smell it," he grinned. "That fresh pavement shop doorway smell?"

"Oh, for God's sake Rob. Is that why you are here?"

Rob put up his hands, "Mea culpa, I don't have anywhere else." He pulled out the lining of the pockets in his trousers. "No money either."

"Where were you after they pulled you in? Why have you turned up again?"

"Apparently I'm no longer a suspect."

"So, what happened?" Rose stared at him, he had clearly been living rough, he was thin, unshaven.

"Rose could we at least have tea, and if possible a snack. I'll tell you everything, I promise. And you don't have to put me up. But if a shower's possible ...." He gave her a hopeful half smile.

"OK, there are towels in the hall cupboard and you can use the blue robe hanging up. I'll wash your clothes, but Rob if you're trying to bluff your way into me letting you stay, or you lie to me, think again."

"OK, Rose, I swear. The whole truth and nothing but."

She picked up the pile of damp clothes he left for her outside the bathroom. She checked the pockets, he was right, he had nothing in the world apart from the old cell phone. Where was his wallet? Rose knew what it was like to sleep on the streets, where anything and everything could and would be taken. It was an experience she wouldn't wish on her worst enemy, well except for Troy perhaps she thought ruefully as she bundled Rob's clothes into the washer dryer.

Rose set about making tea and heating up one of the ready made meals from the supermarket. The food vanished within seconds of Rob sitting at the table.

"You snorted that down. How long since you ate?"

"Two days. I was attacked, roughed up. They took my wallet. I don't know why they didn't take the phone."

"Probably because it's rubbish," quipped Rose.

"Yeah, probably," Rob smiled.

"How do you know the police aren't looking for you now?" Did you contact your solicitor?"

Rob shook his head.

"Why not?"

"Because his office was closed. I left a message." Rose looked baffled.

"Rose, something bad is going on, I don't know what, but I think it started with Sally, then Bakti."

"And then Doctor Reynolds," said Rose slowly.

"Dr Reynolds?"

Rose told Rob about the accident and her visit from DI Chatterton asking what Rose remembered about the man who was run over. "He was a doctor to one of my customers, but he died in hospital," she finished.

"When?"

Rose wrinkled her nose, trying to remember the day Tony told her the accident happened. "He was run over about five days ago."

"So perhaps it was something about his death that made them realise I had nothing to do with Bakti, or Sally."

"But I thought you'd been cleared of Sally's death."

"Yeah, well I thought so too, but they mentioned her again when they questioned me about Bakti."

Rose pulled out a sheet of paper from her desk.

"What are you doing?"

"Writing down everything I know and can remember about what happened to Sally, the day Bakti died and what I know about Dr Reynolds' death. Perhaps there's a pattern."

She finished writing and was back to the same realisation she had had yesterday, all the people who died were connected directly or indirectly to her shop.

"So this pattern Rob, it involves you, well, apart from Dr Reynolds, you knew both Sally and Bakti."

"But Rose. From the pattern you have made, you, well, the shop is more at the centre of this than I am."

Rose put the pen down. "Sally's death was formally recorded as an overdose, Bakti was murdered. And Dr Reynolds was run over but died later in hospital."

"A tragic accident," said Rob.

Hearing those words Rose felt the blood drain from her, her head started to spin and she fell with a crash on the floor.

"Rose, come on let's sit you up." Rob was pulling her towards him as she came to. "What on earth happened? Here, drink some water."

"I'm alright," Rose took a sip of the water and felt her way up onto the sofa. "Tea, please, I need something hot."

"You need to rest too. Look, I know I said I wasn't trying to get you to let me stay, but maybe I can look after you for a couple of days? With it being Christmas and all ..." He looked hopeful and pathetic at the same time. His puppy dog face appealed to her generosity.

Rose hesitated, she remembered all too vividly what had happened to them both the last time, when she had stayed with Rob. "Just over Christmas and New Year then. Except, I mean it Rob, absolutely clean and sober has to be the rule if it's going to work."

"I'm done for good this time Rose. I wish I hadn't started using again, but as you know, relapse can happen. If I think I'm a risk I'll take off. What made you faint?"

Rose shook her head. "It sounds stupid and it can't possibly have anything to do with what's happening, but when you said 'tragic accident' it reminded me of my mother falling down the stairs and hitting her head, I felt as if that had just happened. Do you remember?"

"Yes, yes of course. You phoned her from my house, and she fell trying to get to the phone."

"That's when the drinking really started."

"No Rose, that started when you moved in with Troy. He made you drink, I saw him do that to you, and worse. But you're right, my addiction didn't help matters."

"She really did fall didn't she?"

"Your mother? Well of course she did, there was a huge investigation and reports and everything. Your father wanted it blamed on you, but you were at the other end of the phone, miles away. He did his best to try and prove otherwise."

"He still does blame me," said Rose quietly. "He won't accept she fell. He and I haven't spoken since, even though

I wrote to him, I still write to him, there's rarely a reply, other than criticism. I loved my mother so much. And I miss her terribly."

Rose took a deep breath, but like a surfer caught in a rip current, she lost control and had no choice but to allow the huge howls of anguish to explode from inside.. Her outwardly contained exterior morphed into a soft and vulnerable little girl.

Rob sat with her, stroking her hair, the way he had after her mother Jeannie's death. Back then she had worn it long at Troy's request. After her eye diagnosis, Troy had convinced Rose that a future out of the RAF with him was going to be full of opportunities. It took six months but Troy changed the elfin boyish girl he had first met into a trophy, and for a while, she shone, but as with all trophy hunters, he was always on the lookout for shinier and bigger ones. After two years Rose lost the joie de vivre he had infected her with. The heavy drinking and partying that was Troy's life robbed her of her independence and dignity as she failed to please him, their relationship mirroring the one she had with her father. Rose watched Troy at play with other women, until eventually she couldn't stand it anymore. But even so, it had taken courage to leave, her sense of self esteem was diminished, he had almost convinced her that without him she was future less.

Rob had been Troy's supplier. He was a small fry dealer, failed actor, wannabe musician who didn't fit in mainstream society. His orthodox Jewish family had disowned him when he came out. It was Rob that Rose turned to, grieving the loss of her career, too ashamed to go home to her father, having failed both in her professional and personal life. Two misfits in a world of high achievers. Troy had been furious when he realised Rose had actually left him. He attempted to retrieve her after her mother died. Rose resisted but his persistence paid off and he rewarded her with a shiny extravagant ring. Until the pattern of his behaviour was once again too much for her and The tarnish on his once beloved trophy was almost gone forever. He restored it only to have it shatter into tiny fragments at his behest.

Rob cleared away the detritus from the table and sent Rose to have a bath. "We're both too shattered to think about anything tonight, so let's play Cluedo tomorrow, see if we can figure out what's going on, what the connections are. Bakti didn't kill himself, I certainly didn't kill him, but I'd really like to know who did and why they tried to set me up for it."

Rose nodded. "I doubt we'll get far, but you're right, I can't think about it anymore tonight. Look Rob, I'm sorry if I was hard on you earlier, it's just …"

Rob put his finger to her lips as she was speaking. "It's ok Rose, I get it."

Rose's meticulous and critical thinking brain power was in top form when she woke. She had slept better than she had in weeks, actually since Sally's death. She hadn't realised until now the full impact Sally's death had had on her when she found the girl's body outside the shop. Sally had been Rose's first apprentice when she opened Muffins on Morrison. She had been clean and sober for a year and the social service agency who was supporting Sally had found her a flat at the top of Morrison Street. They had become close but Sally, unlike Trixie, was not reliable and she'd had to let her go. But they had stayed in touch and Rose did what she could to support her, especially after Sally found herself pregnant. After her relapse Sally's baby had gone to stay with Sally's grandmother June. As far as Rose knew, the child was still there. Thank goodness she hadn't had to go into foster care, thought Rose. Would it help to speak to June? Would June even be prepared to talk, Rose wondered, as she put her on one of the lists she was making.

Rose took down some art from one of the walls in the living room and started to pin up the pieces of paper marked with different coloured pens. Rob was still deep asleep under the spare duvet on the sofa bed. It was Christmas morning. There were no presents under the tree, but Rose didn't mind. In an odd way, despite her initial resistance and reluctance to letting Rob stay she was glad he was there.

The sun was rising and the light started to penetrate through the voile curtains. "Merry Christmas" she muttered under her breath and started to hum her favourite carol, In the Bleak Midwinter. Rob stirred, squinting his eyes to adjust to the light as he looked across to where Rose was standing.

"What are you doing?"

"Morning sleepy head, Merry Christmas."

"Yeah, I suppose it is. Merry Christmas Rose. Thanks for the bed."

Rose smiled, 'Well there's even breakfast. Do you want it in bed, or at the table?"

"Table I think, I clearly need to catch up with what you've been doing. Good work it looks from here."

"Well, not really, it's a start, this is the list of people I think we should speak to." She pointed to another sheet. "This is the list of the deceased and this is the list of events or things that stick out in my mind that might be relevant. Please add your own. It's all colour coded too."

"For someone who only has one eye, that's a pretty visual system."

"Yeah, well I've always been a visual thinker. That's what is so hard about this wretched disease. But while I can I'm going to put what sight I have left to good use."

"Do you really miss it?"

"What?"

"Planes and flying, the RAF, your dreams of outer space."

"Yes Rob, I really do. Being told I could do other things, stay in the force, but that I couldn't fly. That day was the worst day of my life."

"Worse than what happened afterwards?"

"Being a drunk and then Troy sending me to prison you mean? Yeah, it was a lot worse than that, because when that happened, he made me believe it was all I deserved."

"I could swing for that guy, if ever I saw him again, I'd have to hit him."

"And he would love it. He hates you almost as much as he hates me, he would have you arrested in a heartbeat."

"Weird how love and hate can look the same. Like my parents who told me they loved me everyday of their lives, until I told them I was gay and then they told me they hated me."

"That's so sad and so stupid Rob and here I am wishing you, a nice Jewish boy, Merry Christmas."

"Ah well, as Jesus was Jewish that's a complex theological conundrum isn't it."

"Do we have time to solve that too?" Rose laughed as she moved over to the kitchen and started to make breakfast. "Pain au chocolat and with scrambled eggs and tomatoes, do you?"

"I'm in heaven," Rob said, as he folded up the bed and tidied the living room.

"Where were you staying before you were arrested? Did you have your own place? I mean. I never knew, you just always popped up when I texted you. Do you have any other clothes?" Rose asked as Rob took off the extra-large T-shirt she had given him to sleep in and he pulled on the clothes she had washed yesterday.

"I sofa surfed most of last year. But that last place, I doubt they'd have kept my stuff. It was just a gym bag with clothes."

"But you had a decent watch and some pretty cool shoes I remember."

"Yeah, well I guess the watch got taken with my wallet and as for everything else, it's only stuff."

"You'll have to rinse through your smalls then until the shops open. I can sub you for undies." Rose smiled as she set out the breakfasts. Something had definitely shifted in her outlook, despite the dark materials they were about to tackle together.

Rob added some events, people and things he thought might be important to Rose's lists. Rose cut some string and wove the pieces together over the lists where people and events, since Sally died, coincided. The hospital was the only location outside Morrison Street. Everything else had occurred on Morrison and in the immediate vicinity.

Sally, June, Rose, Trixie, Tony and Rob were on one list

Bakti, Rob, Trixie, Rose, Tony were on another

Dr Reynolds, Rose, Tony and Babs made up the third list.

"We can't possibly call people today, but what we could do is take a walk, and photograph the different locations. It might jog our memories. What do you think," asked Rose, after they had both stared vacantly at their work for almost half an hour.

"I see Tony is on all the lists," said Rob.

"Well only because he knew everyone, including Bakti, he teaches English as a second language. Surely you don't think he has anything to do with anyone dying."

"No, just an observation that's all. And we're probably missing people too. I mean, Bakti hung out with quite a lot of people. And we haven't included whoever Sally was using to get her gear from."

"Yes, that's true. You have no idea who that might have been? How well do you know any of the students?"

"Trixie probably knows the students better than I do, she and Bakti were members of a group, but when I started going, she stopped. And no, I don't know who Sally was buying from."

"I don't want to get Trixie involved in this. I'm her mentor, supervisor, manager, whatever. I need to keep her safe. She's bright, but she's vulnerable still and spending Christmas at home might not be easy for her. It's the first time she's been back to Fife and spent time with her parents since she left home."

"You have a big heart Rose McLaren. How many people would do what you do for others. And all the muffins you donate to the shelter."

Rose looked down, "Well people were there for me when I needed them. I'm just giving back what was paid forward."

Rose made up some hot chocolate to take on their walk over to Morrison. The sun was out, but it was cold as they made their way through the park and across to Haymarket. "I don't see a point in going to the hospital today do you?"

"No, but it would be good to talk to the paramedics who were on the site."

"True, Tony might be able to help with that."

"Do you want to get him involved, after all isn't his wife dying?"

"Yes, but I think it might help. From what Tony said they feel bad about Dr Reynolds making the home visit, after all if he hadn't been doing that, he wouldn't be dead."

Rob wrinkled his face. "You know that's like the Jesus question you posed earlier, hand of God, fate etcetera. They shouldn't blame themselves for what was an accident, that could have happened anywhere, anytime."

"But that's just it, it wasn't an accident. If what DI Chatterton told me - well hinted at - was true, his death is somehow linked to the others, isn't that what we're assuming, why we are doing this?"

"Yes, you're right."

Rob pointed to the student building opposite her shop, "Look, those two girls, they were the ones who found him. Shall we see if they'll chat to us?"

"Absolutely," said Rose striding purposefully to where the two young women were standing chatting. She was about to ask Rob how he knew the two girls had found Bakti but, as she turned the corner she came face to face with the front of her shop. It was covered in graffiti. "Drug Den, Beware."

"What on earth! Who would do this?" Rose ran to the building, the huge letters were sprayed all over the display window, on the door and on the paintwork below the window. She desperately rubbed her finger against the letters, willing it to rub off. But it didn't. The black writing was permanent, until she could contact a professional with the right tools to help her. She looked at both the neighbouring shops and buildings, there was no graffiti and no new tagging anywhere else that she could see.

"Rose, I'm so sorry."

But Rob's words fuelled her anger and she turned on him. "This is your fault Rob. I should never have had anything to do with you, leave me alone, I never want to see you again. The only drug dealer around here is you. You're the poison, you've always brought me bad luck." She turned away, staring in disbelief at the graffiti.

Rob froze, her words stung. In one way he knew she was right. It was his addiction that had taken her down,. As soon as Rose knew Jeannie had died he should have been there for her, but he had made things worse, introducing her to drugs on top of the alcohol, to relieve her grief. Then Troy had swept in on his white charger and taken her back, "Rose, I'm sorry, look you don't mean that, I know you're angry, but this has nothing to do with me. Please Rose." Rob didn't care that he sounded pathetic, begging her not to abandon him, not to believe he was all rotten, the way Troy was.

Rose just continued to stare at her shop front.

The two students who had been chatting heard the kerfuffle and came over, "Is everything OK?" The young blonde had a slight hint of a different dialect when she spoke, but her English was impeccable. "What happened to your shop?"

"I wish I knew," growled Rose, trying to control her temper. "Did either of you notice this graffiti before this morning?"

They looked at each other and shook their heads. "Sorry, no, we wouldn't have noticed now, except for your argument."

Rob took the opportunity to change the subject, "You were friends with Bakti?" He asked them.

"Yes, you too I think. I saw you, before right?"

"Yes, yes you did."

"You were …" she put her head on one side, "close, I think, that is what you say here. You were close."

Rob's eyes filled with tears. He was still reeling from the things Rose had said. Remembering Bakti, his emotions overwhelmed him and he broke down.

Rose put her hand out to Rob. "I'm sorry Rob. I shouldn't have said those things. Come on, let's go inside, we can at least get warm. Would you two be able to come inside too. Rob and I, well we have some questions about Bakti, and you were both there when he was found. Is that right?"

"Yes." The girls nodded. "We will come, tell you what we know," said the blonde.

There was a piece of paper with letters printed in red felt pen, lying on the mat inside the shop as Rose opened the door. It said, "*This is Not Over*".

The paper was crumpled as if the note had been written on a piece of scrap as an afterthought, or the writer had changed their minds, screwed the paper up and then changed it back again. Rose picked it up and handed it to Rob.

"Better not touch it, you never know there might be prints," Rob said.

Rose shrugged, that message, those words, where had she heard them before? She placed the paper on the counter and then busied herself, trying to distract herself from the shock, making hot drinks for everybody.

Rob started to ask the girls about the day Bakti died.

It was the other girl who spoke. She was Spanish, and her name was Teresa. She had been in Bakti's cohort in the English language classes, Tony was their teacher.

"It was horrible. I went to his room, he was usually waiting for me in the hallway, but he wasn't there and he was not picking up his messages. It looked like he hadn't been online for a while, which was not like Bakti, he was always messaging, even in class. The door was open so I went in and saw him, he was hanging next to the bed, he had used the light fitting. There was a stool kicked over, but he must have stood on the bed too." She put her hands over her face as she recalled the scene. The blonde girl put her arm over Teresa's shoulder.

"It's true, Teresa was screaming when she called me on the phone. I didn't know what she was saying, except to come to Bakti's room. When I got there Teresa was sitting on the floor. Bakti was hanging. It was me who called 999."

"I was stupid," Teresa said, "I should have checked he was alive, but I froze, I did nothing to help him. Maybe it's my fault he is dead."

"No, Teresa, you were in shock. Tell her please, it isn't her fault."

Rob leaned across the table. "Teresa, of course this was not your fault. Someone else did this to Bakti, someone evil."

Rose came back with a tray of tea and some of the Father Christmas biscuits. Their jolly iced faces seemed out of place given the conversation, but it was all the baking that she had left.

"Who would want to hurt Bakti? He was so nice, so popular."

"Was there anyone new that you saw Bakti with, anything odd about his behaviour?" Rose asked.

"No. He was worried about his father coming because, well, you know," she looked at Rob, "you know why."

Rob nodded. "But that doesn't have anything to do with this. And Bakti would not have committed suicide."

"How do they know he was murdered?" Teresa asked. "I only heard it from the news. The police did not tell me this."

"We don't know either," replied Rose.

"Well, we still don't have much to go on do we?" Rob said as Rose locked up and they walked back to her flat. Their enthusiasm for taking photographs or doing anything else had waned after Rose called the police about the graffiti, and taken the photographs of the outside of the shop the police asked for. It sounded as if it wasn't going to be a priority. The police had told them to leave the note where it was.

"Nope, we don't. If only it wasn't Christmas Day, we could call some of the others."

"Let me look at the picture you took of that note shoved through the door."

They both studied the image on Rose's phone. There was something disturbing about the wording, a threat. That wording "*This is not over*", was it to do with the murders or something else? Rose shivered.

"Call that DI," Rob urged.

"But it's already reported and they didn't seem to want to do anything about it today."

" But the DI, he might think the note is also important. And perhaps he would give us some information about Bakti, and what happened to Dr Reynolds, how come they think his death is suspicious when he died at the hospital."

"Didn't they say anything to you when they questioned you, about how Bakti died I mean."

"Yeah, but it didn't make sense They said overdose, but he was found hanging to make it look like a suicide and said I'd done that to cover up I'd supplied him with bad gear. Then they started asking questions about Sally again. Intimating , that I knew it was bad and didn't care. I was really scared, I thought I was going to be banged up forever, that's why I had to run."

"So how did you find out they weren't looking for you anymore?"

"I know people."

Rose accepted the lack of information at face value. She knew Rob wouldn't tell her anymore about his connection to the darker side of Edinburgh. "OK Rob. So, although we don't know for sure, let's assume that whoever the killer is, used a drug on Dr Reynolds, that he also died of an overdose. Could that mean someone at the hospital is involved? Someone with medical knowledge how to make an overdose look like an accident, like Sally?"

"But in that case why try to make Bakti look like a suicide?"

"True, we're just going round in circles aren't we?"

"It does have to be the same person doesn't it?"

"Well, unless you think there's a gaggle of nutters out there, looks that way to me, and how are you and shop tied into it all?"

Rose shrugged. She put her head on his shoulder as they sat in silence mulling over what they knew and didn't know.

The church bell rang out. It was 6pm. Rose stretched out onto the couch. "I hate myself, I want a gin and tonic."

Rob got up and walked over to the kitchen. "Any chance of some dinner? Take your mind off other things."

"There's tons, do you fancy cooking? I think I'd like to take a bath, turn things over in my mind differently. I have a niggle, as if there's a clue staring us in the face, but I can't see it."

Rob busied himself rummaging through the groceries Rose had bought. It would be an unusual Christmas Dinner, but that wasn't new. He hadn't had a normal one since Rose and he had shared that flat, before booze took over. There had been plenty of gin and tonics that year, more gin than tonic from what he remembered. Christmas shopping had meant a trolley full of bottles and a little bit of food. And then came the drugs. He had known they would, as sure as night follows day, but Rose hadn't tried it before. The experience had almost killed her, Rob had called the ambulance and it was touch and go, but she made it.. Then Troy had wormed his way back,, helped put her back together, promised her the world, but of course that had been rubbish. He had tried to get Rob arrested , but that hadn't worked so well.

"Mmmm, smells delicious," said Rose as she came back into the living room. Her hair was wet and she hadn't dressed, she was wrapped in a towel. Her upper arms were tattooed with a mandala and some writing quotes.

"You got some new ones I see," Rob tilted his head towards her.

"Yeah, when I opened the shop, my fresh start," she said looking at the quote from Winnie the Pooh, written between her elbow and her shoulder. *"Always remember you're braver than you believe, stronger than you seem and smarter than you think."*

"That's a bit cheesy for you, and you've always been brave."

"I was once, but Troy, going to prison, both knocked my confidence. I can't believe the way I had just signed whatever Troy put in front of me without checking first. Three months before I was due out he came to visit me. When he wrote and asked for permission, I should have said no but I was curious. What on earth could he want? Do you know what he said, did I tell you this already?"

"No, you didn't, you have never spoken about him to me, since that time, until now."

"It was extraordinary. He came with another engagement ring. It was huge, bigger than the first, and must have cost a fortune. He said surely now I realised we were meant to be together. That's why he had to take drastic measures, for my safety, he didn't expect me to end up in prison when I was charged. I asked him to confess to making everything up, but he said I was imagining it, that what I had done was wrong and he forgave me. I remember just sitting there in stunned silence. And then I laughed, quite hysterically I think because one of the officers came over to see if everything was alright, she thought I was crying. Then I started yelling 'get out', I think I swore at him. And, then he said - and I think this is what made me think about all of this just now - *'It's not over, it will never be over*.' So, whoever did the graffiti has a long term grudge with me. Like Troy."

"Wait, you think Troy's behind this?"

"No, of course not, that would be ridiculous, after all it's been over four years since I saw him and set up the shop. He did me a favour, I couldn't have done that without learning baking in prison."

"Who needs university?"

Rose smiled at Rob's dig. "Not quite what I meant but, yeah, honestly that programme saved me. It gave me hope, to start over."

"And then I came along and ruined it," said Rob.

"No, no you didn't and I'm sorry for what I said earlier. But you know what they say at the meetings is right. Friends in recovery can be the best support for each other and the worst enemy."

"We need to find who Sally was buying from," said Rob.

"Agreed, that's on your list, can you follow up with that?"

"Yeah, I think so. Now call the DI, tell him what's happened."

Rose picked up her phone and dialled but her call went straight to voicemail. "Not surprising given it's late on Christmas Day. Let's put this to one side, can we watch a Christmas film, be normal?"

"We are normal, just a bit more edge than most folks around here."

They were halfway through watching Elf when DI Chatterton returned Rose's call. He wanted to meet, he sounded concerned. Rose agreed to meet him at the shop in the morning at 10am. "So much for a five day break," she grumbled.

Chapter Five

December 26th

"Let's meet at Marks on Princes Street, we can get you some underwear and a shirt," said Rose as they left the flat together. Rob was heading off to try and find out who Sally had been buying from and Rose to meet the DI. They parted company outside the building, Rose cut through the park and Rob continued on down the street. Neither of them noticed the hooded male sitting in the car opposite.

As soon as they were far enough away the man slipped out of the car and let himself into the building. His access was swift, he had a key. No passer-by would have realised his entry wasn't as a bona fide resident. He paused in the hallway, checking the stairs. He seemed to know his way around and once he was satisfied he wouldn't be seen he ran silently up the stairs, two at a time and turned the key into the lock. He was dressed in black from head to toe, there were no markings or logos on his tight-fitting clothes. His hands were covered in fine black calf leather gloves. The layout of the flat was familiar to him as he made his way from the vestibule into the living room and kitchen. He looked inside the cupboard under the sink, paused and then retreated into Rose's bedroom. It was a bright room, sparsely decorated. The large wardrobe and old-fashioned dresser stood opposite the window, with her bed facing them. The only other furniture was a wooden ottoman and a bedside table. He opened the wardrobe, then each of the drawers in the dresser, fingering the clothes but being careful not to disturb the well organised contents. He paused and then moved over to the ottoman. It too was well organised, filled with photographs and memorabilia from Rose's RAF days and her childhood. He smiled as he perused the images of Rose in uniform. The ottoman stood about six inches from the ground. He put his hands underneath. The surface was smooth. Carefully taking out everything inside and putting them in an orderly sequence, he turned it over and fished in his inner jacket for the bundle of tiny clear sealed bags. He laid each of the bags on the bottom of the ottoman and taped them over so they were flat and could not be seen when the ottoman was right side up. The whole process was neat, methodical and fast, the contents put back in exactly the order he had taken them out. He was about to leave when he went back over to the dresser. He pulled some hairs from the hairbrush and put them in a bag from the pocket where the other bags had been. Zipping up the jacket he let himself out of the flat, carefully locking the door and re-checking the stairwell in case anyone else was up and about. His mission had taken him less than ten minutes.

.oOo.

DI Chatterton was already outside the shop when Rose arrived. He was studying the graffiti. Rose unlocked and showed him the note she had found. He looked at it carefully, before he sealed it into an evidence bag. "Who has touched it?" he asked.

"Well only me, Rob told me to put it down, so no one else, apart from whoever put it there."

"We will need your fingerprints."

"Really? Don't you already have them?"

"Ah yes, of course. How remiss of me. You've been watching too much TV, Miss. We'll need a new set."

Rose wasn't sure if he was joking or not. The DI was hard to read. His manner was remote, he was English, more London than county, and somewhere in his late fifties she supposed, but apart from that she couldn't tell very much else about him.

"This Rob, how well do you know him? How did you meet?"

"Why do you want to know, I thought he had been cleared of any suspicion."

"That would need a jury, what makes you say that?"

He was playing cat and mouse with her, she could tell. The DCI who had arrested her had done the same, until she had tired of the game, stopped protesting her innocence and agreed to plead guilty for a reduced sentence. Like that had worked. Even her brief had been shocked how harsh the judge had been on her. Everyone was convinced, by pleading guilty, she would get a suspended sentence, especially as her accuser had also written mitigating circumstances, implicating she had stolen from him to feed her drug habit and named Rob.

"We met after I left the RAF. He was an acquaintance of my then boyfriend, who I was living with."

"Mr Troy Ferguson?"

Rose nodded.

"Did Rob deal drugs back then, apart from his walk-on roles on the telly I mean."

"I didn't know that about him, I just thought he and Troy were friends, but Troy treated him like rubbish. We used to get along, I didn't like many of Troy's other friends. Rob made me laugh."

"You were how old by then?"

"I was twenty-six. I moved out of Troy's; he was being unfaithful and I couldn't handle it. Rob had a spare room, so I moved in there. But he was going through a rough time, his family had found out he was gay and he was drinking a lot, that's when I found out about the drugs as well. I phoned my mum, I was going to ask her if I could come home but …" Rose stopped, her eyes welled up with tears and she couldn't breath.

The DI finished her sentence for her. "But she died."

"Yes! For God's sake why on earth are you asking me about all of this, when obviously you already know my story. Excuse me." Rose headed to the toilet to calm herself down. When she came back another officer was there, he was examining the graffiti on the outside of the building.

"Look, I'm sorry I didn't mean to upset you, it's just sometimes better to hear someone's story first hand, rather than what's written about them."

"Yes, probably, I am sure that what's written about me isn't very flattering."

"Well, it seems that you had several run-ins with us before you managed to turn things around."

"Yes, drunk and disorderly, possession, public affray. That's all in the past. I have my business and I'm going to make a real success of it. I was doing fine until all of this, whatever this is, started. I want to know what really happened to Sally, to that student, and the doctor."

The DI nodded. "I can't say anything about an ongoing investigation, but we will need your statement, can you come down and do that, perhaps tomorrow?"

"So, do you think this is tied in with everything else?"

"Too soon to say. My advice would be to keep away from your friend Rob. He seems like trouble."

The DI made to leave but just as he was out of the door he turned to ask something else. "You mentioned the shop isn't very profitable, how do you keep going?"

"I can cover my costs, I just don't make the sort of money that giant tech does," Rose snapped. "I'll come by tomorrow, for the statement. "Thank you, morning would be best" said the DI.

"Infuriating man," Rose muttered to herself as the door closed finally, cursing herself for not asking if she could have the graffiti removed. The clean up and repainting claim was going to impact her insurance premium, but she couldn't re-open in the New Year with the shop in this state. Everything was challenging her resolve to stay clean, she could feel the gremlins clawing at her insides, making her doubt herself. Rose pulled up the sleeve of her sweater and looked at the tattoo Rob had noticed last night. He was right, it was cheesy, but the words were what she needed to remind herself to stay strong and trust herself. She looked around, everything on the inside had been cleaned after they closed on Christmas Eve. There was just the floor to do, but not much point in that if painters are coming she thought. They'll have their dirty boots everywhere. She looked at her phone, it was too early to head to meet Rob. The sun was shining, focus on the sun, she told herself. She would take a walk up Morrison, maybe call briefly on Tony and Babs to say Merry Christmas and see if they had any news that could help regarding what had happened to Doctor Reynolds at the hospital.

Rose was about to leave when she saw Teresa banging on the door.

"Come in," Rose beckoned.

"Hello Rose, is it ok, are you busy?"

"No, it's fine. How are you?"

"I'm troubled, worried is that what you say?"

Teresa's face was serious, her eyes looked puffy as if she had been crying.

"Yes, that's what we say, what about? Is it Bakti?"

"Yes, but afterwards. I remembered something that I saw."

"Shall I make tea, and you can tell me if you want."

"Do you have coffee?"

Rose smiled, "Yes of course, coffee."

Teresa was fiddling with her hair when Rose came back with two steaming mugs of coffee. "Where's your friend today?"

Teresa shrugged, "Her name is Andrea, we had a row."

Rose pulled a face, "I'm sorry, that's too bad. But what is it you have remembered?"

"Well there was someone I didn't recognise, the day Bakti died. He seemed to be there a lot that day, walking near Bakti's room in the morning and then later, after the police came, I saw him watching everything. I haven't seen him since. Andrea said it was nothing, but I am not so sure."

"I'm guessing you haven't told the police then?"

"No, the policeman, he came earlier, then I saw him talking to you. But I didn't say anything. Andrea told me not to get more involved, she said if I told them this they would always be bothering me."

"What did he look like, this man?"

"I didn't see his face. He had a bag with him, like a gym bag."

"A gym bag? What colour?"

"Dark, black I think, like his clothes."

Rose made a mental note to ask Rob what colour his missing gym bag had been, even though this was probably a coincidence. "Is there anything else you can remember, logos or what type of shoes.?"

"No everything was black, I think that's why I noticed him, because usually people have something like a, as you say, logo on their clothing. There was nothing. Is it helpful, for you and your friend I mean?"

"Well possibly. Can I ask you something?"

"Yes, of course."

"Rob, my friend who was here yesterday. Did you also see him on the day Bakti died?"

"Yes, he was here, outside your shop, but earlier, I was coming back from class, about 2 o'clock I think. I waved at him, but he didn't see me."

"And this man you saw, did he see Rob or seem to know him?"

"I don't know, I didn't see them together and the time was different."

"Thanks Teresa. I hope you and Andrea make up soon, it's not worth falling out over this. Thank you for telling me though. Do you want me to mention it to the police?"

"Thanks, but I think I should say it. Maybe, I will think about it. Maybe Andrea is right and he is no one, not important. I will buy her some beer, she will forgive me for sure!"

Teresa's face was happy and smiling by the time she left, lightened by sharing her story and the thought of beer with Andrea. Rose washed away the cups, locked up and headed off to Princes Street to meet Rob, it was too late to call in and see Tony now.

Princes Street was crowded, the sun and the Boxing Day sales had lured shoppers on the hunt for bargains from their living rooms. Rob was already outside Marks when she arrived.

"Hello, any luck?"

Rob shook his head. "No, the flat I went to, where I was staying before has been cleared out and locked up. Looks like there might have been a fire inside, but there was no way in. I talked to someone else, but he didn't know anything about Sally. He said there had been someone sniffing around, they thought he might be an undercover cop and that my name had come up as a snitch."

"Well that's good information isn't it. Did he say what the suspected cop looked like?"

"I didn't ask. Why?"

"Teresa, from yesterday, she came over to the shop and told me about a man she saw, the day Bakti died. He was dressed in black, he had a gym bag with him. I wondered, do you think it could have been yours?"

"Rose, there are thousands of men with gym bags in this city. How did you even make that connection?"

Rose shrugged, "Come on let's get you kitted out then."

Rob wrinkled his nose, "In here?"

"Yes Rob, good old M & S, they have knickers that never let you down."

While Rob was shopping Rose looked around in the men's clothing section. Teresa was right, even here at Marks all the outer wear, t-shirts, shoes and casual trousers had a logo or something on them. She couldn't find anything completely plain.

"What were you looking for?" Rob asked as they queued up to pay for Rob's purchases. Rose described the man that Teresa had seen.

"She saw you outside the shop, Tony saw you too. What were you doing there Rob?"

"I thought I told you before, I was waiting for Bakti. We were supposed to meet after class at around 1.30, then he sent another text to say he was still in class and he would meet me later."

"Wait - what time did the second text come in?"

"It was after 2.00, well just before you sent me a text anyway."

"But he was already dead by then, because I sent Trixie to take a break, that must have been about 2.30. Didn't the police check all this with you?"

"Yes, but Bakti's phone was missing, it was part of their evidence against me, that I had sent the text from him because I didn't know his body had already been found."

"If he was killed at around 1.30pm when he was supposed to be meeting you, do you think that earlier text really was from him? Did someone else text you, to put you in the location at the right time, so you would be a suspect?"

Rob pulled out his phone and started scrolling back through his messages, looking for the ones from Bakti. "Look, I didn't realise this until now." Rob showed Rose the two texts arranging the meetings and then earlier ones. "See, he always used to include this little cartoon frog when he sent me a message. These last two don't have the frog."

"What other evidence did the police have when they questioned you?"

"They said they had my DNA, and a witness, I don't know who that was. My solicitor felt it was tenuous, but the police presented a strong case and, because of my history, what happened to you, I was scared."

"I think we need to talk to the girls again, well Teresa at least. And let's go back via Tony and Babs, I want to check in on them anyway, but we really need to know what happened to Doctor Reynolds and why whatever happened to him seemed to give the police reason to realise you weren't guilty of killing Bakti."

As they turned the corner into the crescent where Tony and Babs lived they saw Babs being carried on a stretcher into an ambulance.

"Tony?" Rose called as she ran towards him. "What's happened?"

"Babs isn't doing well, she caught a cold and now she can hardly breathe, they're going to put her on oxygen, they can't do that here, she needs monitoring."

"I'll come to the hospital, meet you there."

"Thanks Rose. I appreciate it." Tony climbed into the back of the ambulance. His face crumpled with worry about his wife.

"Well it gives you a reason to be at the hospital," said Rob. "Sorry if that sounds mean."

"No, it doesn't, I hated myself for offering knowing I had another reason. But I do care about them, so I would be going anyway."

"Don't they have children?"

"No, there was a son , but he left home, it all seems very sad. . They haven't seen him for years. Look I'll see you later, do you fancy trying to follow up with June, Sally's mum, or see the girls?"

"Neither, I'm going to try and find out about that supposed undercover. Can you take these bags, I don't want to take them where I'm going."

.oOo.

The hospital was busy, Rose asked the taxi to drop her off at Emergency but there was a line of cars all looking for parking and she decided to walk. She passed three paramedics, two men and a woman, it looked like they were on a break.

"Hi, sorry to be a bother but just wondering if any of you were the responders to that hit-and-run on Morrison, an elderly man was hit on the crossing?"

The group looked at each other and shook their heads. "You'd have to check with the admin, if you know the date and time, they can easily tell you. But if you are a journalist you'll be out of luck?"

"No, I'm a friend." Rose's face flushed with the lie.

"Yeah right hen and I'm the Queen of Sheba," one of the men replied. "You might want to be careful, curiosity killed the cat and all that," he said. His voice was hard, without humour, the other two laughed.

Rose hurried away, feeling unsettled.

Babs was already on a ward when Rose found Tony. He was waiting in the hall outside the room whilst the medical team settled his wife.

"So she caught a cold and this happened."

"Yeah, stupid isn't it, but it went straight to her chest. The problem is her treatment is limited because of the cancer drugs, which is why they wanted to get her in as soon as possible. She's been really down since Dr Reynolds died. She's been stressed, the police have been asking her too many questions. All irrelevant, I told them to leave her alone."

"Who is her new doctor, since her old one just died, I mean?" Rose knew the question had been clumsily put, she wanted to see if Tony knew anything about Doctor Reynolds without making it obvious like she had with the paramedics. But Tony didn't seem to notice.

"Just an emergency locum, he was very good, but it wasn't the same. Old Reynolds, well he was special."

"Do they know what happened, why they are treating his death as suspicious?"

"What, what do you mean?"

Rose sighed, "Sorry, I thought you knew."

"No, I have been speaking to the police, but they didn't say anything else or that something had happened here, it was more about how well we knew him. That car, the one that didn't stop, well I thought it was just a hit-and-run."

Rose told him what DI Chatterton had told her, and how she and Rob were trying to connect the dots between Sally, Bakti and Doctor Reynolds.

"You mustn't Rose, it's too dangerous, if there is a connection, let the police do their job. They'll find whoever is responsible."

Rose wished she had Tony's faith in the system. "We're just finding out what we can, of course we'll tell the police anything we find out. Rob spent almost two months hiding when they had him down as the main suspect for Sally, so he's particularly keen to make sure no one connects him with what's been going on. And the graffiti over my shop."

"What graffiti?"

Rose explained what they had found on Christmas Day, and about meeting the two students. "Did you see anyone suspicious, someone dressed in black, holding a gym bag?"

"No Rose, anything that I thought would help I'd have told the police. But of course until now, I had no idea that what happened to that poor young student and Doctor Reynolds might be connected."

"And Sally too."

"Och, poor Sally. She was trying so hard to put everything right for her daughter and her. It was a tragedy when she relapsed."

"You know, there's something about that. Her relapse I mean. She was doing well, and suddenly boom, there she was dead outside the shop."

"And your friend, wasn't he supposed to be the one who she got the drugs from?"

"She didn't get that stuff from Rob, she'd stopped buying from him and, I know it sounds weird to say this, Rob is very honest. He only sells to people he knows can handle it, and he makes sure it's safe."

"Trixie tells a different story, did you know that Rose?"

"How do you know so much about it and what Trixie says?"

"I was young once, and I do work at the University, I see what goes on, who's clean, who's not and I keep my eyes open, in case anyone is in trouble. We all do, us oldies on staff. I saw Trixie shouting at Rob, it was before Sally died. She told him to get lost, she accused him of hurting her friend, something like, 'I'll never forgive you for Michelle, you know what you did.' I'm not sure if those were her exact words but she was really angry. He looked quite frightened when she yelled that, as if he was worried someone else had heard. He didn't see me, I was in the stairwell. Be careful around him Rose."

Rose nodded, "I will, but I have known him for a long time. He's vulnerable too."

A nurse came bustling out of the ward to get Tony. "You can go in now, she's comfortable, sleeping, but you can sit with her."

"I'll let you go Tony, is there anything I can do for you two?"

"Yes Rose there is, by being careful, please." His eyes held her in his. They were kind. She wished her own father would look at her like that.

Rose smiled and nodded, "I will, and I'll come back to check in on you and see how Babs is doing."

She continued back along the corridor. There was a reception and clinical administration station just before the lift. The young woman sitting there looked slightly bored; she was staring into space as Rose approached her. "Not too busy today then?"

The question made the woman jumpy. "What, oh yes, well it is. Sorry I was lost in thought. How can I help?"

"Umm, I'm a niece of a patient who came in just before Christmas. He died, I'm just wondering who I should speak to about his records, cause of death, it's all been a bit confusing."

"Name?" The woman started typing the information Rose gave to her into the computer. Her eyes scanned the information that had come up. Rose leaned over the desk, but the monitor was angled so that no one else could read what was on the screen.

"I'm sorry, that information is not available. You will have to speak to either the police or the coroner's office."

"OK, thanks," said Rose, cursing herself. That was twice now she had failed to get any information and if anybody started asking questions about who she was, and why she was asking, she knew they would remember her. Why had she worn the red beret, it wasn't exactly discreet. She was about to turn away from the desk when the young woman got up.

"Loo break," she whispered to Rose as she rushed past.

Rose looked around, there was no one there, was there a chance the clerk had forgotten to close down the screen? Rose's heart was beating fast as she slipped behind the desk. Rose tapped the mouse and the screen lit up, she couldn't believe it, there was the record. She pulled out her phone and took a quick image of the screen. It wasn't very clear but it would do. She could hear footsteps coming from around the corner, she ducked down hoping it wasn't the admin woman back already. But whoever it was passed by without a second look. As the footsteps faded she knew she daren't stay a minute longer, even though she longed to see more, she needed to go.

The lift down to the main floor took her past another admin station. "Do you know where I might find out which ambulance was dispatched to an accident?" Rose asked the clerk. He nodded and pointed to the corridor behind her. "First left, they might know, but you're better talking to admissions. They would have the names."

"Thanks," said Rose. But she decided not to chance her luck any further. Rose called Rob but he didn't pick up. She sent him a text. *I have some news, see you back at the flat in an hour? My turn to cook.*

Rose decided to make a paella, but she was out of saffron. She was sure the little grocery near her flat would have it, they seemed to sell every spice imaginable in there. The watery sun was almost set over the park by the time she had shopped and let herself into the flat. She gasped as she opened the door, the piece of pink folded paper she always put at the top of her door whenever she left just in case someone got in was lying on the mat. The folded paper was a trick she had learned in prison, it had saved her from a surprise attack more than once.

"Rob?" she called, reaching into the tiny closet in the vestibule for a walking pole.

She stayed still, barely breathing, her sharp ears listening carefully, but there was no sound. Rose walked carefully through each of the rooms but nothing seemed to have been disturbed. Even so, the pink paper didn't lie, someone, at sometime earlier, had been there, and she doubted it had been Rob. She picked up her phone to call the DI about her intruder, then thought better of it. She wanted to piece what she knew together before she talked to him. And what would she say, after all the only clue someone had been there was the piece of pink paper.

Rose studied the medical notes from the photo she had taken at the hospital. The injuries were not consistent with cause of death. A note had been added later, a pathology report showing traces of morphine. Cause of death to be determined.

"Morphine?" Rose said aloud as she re-read the notes. She made two new lists.

Graffiti - refers to drugs

Doctor Reynolds - Morphine

Sally - Overdose (Morphine?)

Bakti - Overdose (Morphine?)

For the second list Rose divided the paper into two parts. Heading one side 'witnesses' and the other side 'suspects'. Under suspects she wrote 'stranger in black' (Bakti) and underneath that 'car driver' (Reynolds). The problem was no one seems to have remembered the model of the car from what Tony had said when he talked to the police. Despite several witnesses, none of them had been able to get a number plate, it was too dark. And there was no CCTV footage that helped. Rose wrote down what she knew from the DI and what Tony had told her they knew about the hit and run. It happened just after 4pm, Dr Reynolds was carrying muffins and using the crossing further up Morrison. Why had he done that Rose wondered? Her shop was on the same side as the turning into the Crescent where Tony and Babs lived. The crossing was taking him away from their flat, not towards it. Sally's old flat, above the games cafe, looked out over that crossing, but why would Dr Reynolds be going there? Rose put the paper to one side and repeated the detailed analysis from what she remembered when Sally's body was found.

Rose had assumed, at the time, Sally had seen the light on and was trying to get Rose's attention when she fell against the door. But now it seemed someone else might have contrived to make it look that way, and propped Sally up by the door so Rose would find her. Someone who must have seen Rose working late. Di one of the passers by call the ambulance. Why didn't they knock on the door?

What did that mean, someone knew she was there late, was spying on her? What about the graffiti? Anyone could have done that knowing she was closed until after the holidays. And whoever had broken into the flat today, was that the same person? Rose's head was spinning as she thought about the various situations. She jumped at the sound of the buzzer. It was Rob.

He looked terrible, his clothes were bloody and torn.

"What on earth has happened?"

"Can I shower and tell you afterwards? Sorry Rose, I think I've put my feet into a hornets' nest and stirred it up."

"Someone's been here today."

"What!"

"Look, get showered and clean up, then we can swap stories. Your new stuff is on the couch."

"You first," said Rob as he sat down to the steaming bowl of paella Rose had prepared. She handed him the notes she had been writing out before he came back.

"Morphine, well that's very interesting," he said after taking everything in. "Both Sally and Bakti were injected with morphine, that's how they died."

"How do you know? Tell me what happened to you."

"I don't know directly, but after I left you, I went East to see someone, I can't tell you who and she …"

"She?" interrupted Rose.

"Yeah, women can be criminals too, didn't you know that? Shall I go on?"

Rose was taken aback by how hard Rob had responded and spoken to her. She didn't like it, but she wanted him to tell her, so she played along. Acted contrite. "Sorry."

He nodded. "Well apparently your little business has got somebody upset. She didn't know who, but she did know that it was somebody connected to a new drugs cartel, they have a lab and sell to clubs; they also deal morphine and have a connection to the hospital, a paramedic is the go-between."

Rose's stomach turned. "Damn" she muttered.

"What is it?"

"I spoke to three paramedics today, one was pretty rude, in a way. They'd certainly know who I was if anyone asked them, I wasn't exactly inconspicuous while I was at the hospital."

"I gathered that by the information you managed to get, sneak peeking at medical records is an offence. You're lucky no one saw you doing that."

"What if Doctor Reynolds was not the saint Tony and Babs think he is, maybe he was involved and crossed them somehow, that's what got him killed. I wondered why he was on the wrong part of Morrison."

"What do you mean?"

"Well look," she drew on the back of one of the papers, "this is the shop, this is where he was run over, and this is where Tony and Babs live. He was up by where Sally used to live, but he was supposed to be going to Tony and Babs."

"Right, that is odd. Could be, but then there's Bakti. He didn't do drugs, well nothing serious, just weed."

"So why was he killed?

Rob shook his head.

"When did you get beaten up?"

"It was afterwards when I was leaving. They could have done a lot worse, but someone else called out and then they ran off."

"Save it for later, that sounds like a threat. Like the note, *It's not over*, or whatever they wrote."

"Look Rose, I think I had better leave here, perhaps you were right. Someone's out for me and I brought them to your door."

"Or, it's the other way around, and I'm the target who has got you involved."

"Possibly. I think you need to tell the DI about the break in, and what I found out, only you can't tell them how."

Rose sat silently looking over the notes she had made. "I can't tell the DI what I did at the hospital, and how can I explain how I know what you found out? I think we need to carry on Rob, and if we find evidence that points to who is behind everything, then we tell them. In the meantime, we have to hope that they are doing their job properly and get there first before anything happens to anyone else. I will feel safer with you here to be honest. Although Tony warned me off. Why were you and Trixie yelling at each other in front of the University?"

Rob rolled his eyes. "When?"

"Must have been before Sally died, and Trixie only came in July, so July or August I suppose."

Rob pursed his lips and then nodded, "Oh yeah, I remember, I didn't know she was working for you when I ran into her. You and I hadn't been in touch that much and I was on my way over, to buy muffins in fact, when she saw me. She had no idea I knew you and started banging on about how her life was changing and that she didn't need someone like me hanging around. When she told me where she was working, look I'm sorry Rose, I told her I knew you and that -." He hung his head.

"What, what else did you say?"

"I told her about you being in prison."

Rose stood up, "You absolute bastard Rob. How could you?"

He held up his hands, "Yeah, it wasn't my finest moment, but I couldn't stand how high and mighty she was being with me and how you were supposed to be all that. I was the devil and you were a saint."

Rose walked away, into her bedroom. She lay down on the soft lilac duvet and stared at the ceiling. In the twelve years she had known Rob they had got drunk together, used together, gone to meetings together and he had been there for her when she was in prison. He wrote, came to see her, had been partly responsible for encouraging her to apply for the business grant. She had supported him when his family rejected him, as her father had rejected her after her mother died, and when his acting or musical career failed to thrive, or he was jilted by a lover and he relapsed big time. That had been two years ago, a year after she celebrated opening the shop. To all intents and purposes Rob was her best friend and at one time she had thought she was his. No-one had believed her side of the story, apart from Rob. But he had betrayed her, the one thing she had asked him never to say to anyone, because the fact that she had been in prison was her story and one day she was going to prove she hadn't deserved to be there.

Chapter Six

Eight Years Earlier

"Sign here, and then we're done for the day. How about dinner at The Lobster Pot?" Troy was sitting on the desk as Rose completed signing the documents. The restaurant he suggested was expensive, one of his favourites.

She shrugged, "That's kind but you've done enough. Honestly, Troy, giving me a home, this job, you don't know how much it means to me. I thought I was on the scrap heap when I came out of rehab the last time. Waking up in that god awful shelter and being kicked out until 5pm, having to apply again night after night just to be able to sleep indoors. You're my boss now, let's keep it that way."

Troy shifted closer towards her. She could feel the tension building up in her body whenever he got too close. The attraction to him had never worn off, despite the affairs he had had when they were together, after they had become engaged. He always seemed to be able to reel her back in, but why he had wanted to even after she had become a street junkie, she still hadn't figured out. He had paid the rent on a tiny flat for her until she could pay for it herself out of the wages from the job he had created for her. But she had resisted his overtures indicating he wanted to start everything up again romantically and he had seemed to accept that until recently.

Troy had built a successful investment business offering current and former military service personnel the opportunity to grow their pensions. He sold various life insurance policies and offered a good return on the investments he suggested. He had good connections and his company was worth a lot of money. He was trusted by the great and the good, he had built his reputation on charm and hard work, but he played hard too. He liked the finer things in life which is why Rose couldn't figure out why he still wanted her. He could have any woman he wanted. The first time she left him, she had run away to Rob's. She had no plan or money of her own. After her mother died, Rose and Rob slid together down the slippery pole of addiction. They were kicked out of the house Rob had been renting and Rose ended up rough sleeping on the streets of Glasgow. Troy paid for her rehab and when she was clean he moved her back in with him. When he proposed three months later, Rose accepted. Troy persuaded her that a drink every so often wouldn't be a problem, but it was a problem and she couldn't stop. Troy paid for more rehab and once again persuaded her that she would be fine so long as she was with him. And she was for a while, until she couldn't take the put downs and the affairs any longer.

That time after she left he allowed her to fall, and she fell hard. She lived on the streets for almost a year, she was arrested for stealing, fighting and possession. When it looked like she would be locked up Troy posted bail on the condition she went back to rehab. After that she moved into a women's shelter. And that was when he had offered her the chance to change her future again, this time by working for him and living on her own, somewhere safe.

"Rose, even colleagues have dinner together. I promise, it's just dinner, no big deal." Troy held his hands up and cocked his head to one side. She could feel him reeling her in again.

"Alright but no alcohol, for me anyway."

"Of course, I'll book a table."

After they were seated at the corner table Troy had booked he took a long time running through the list of exceptional wines The Lobster Pot offered, reading out the names and savouring each one as if he were tasting them. He settled on a Chateauneuf du Pape. "Are you sure, Rose?" he asked as the maltre d' uncorked the bottle and poured an amount for him to taste.

"Yes, absolutely." Rose picked up the glass of tonic water with lime and turned her head towards the view of the Forth Bridge. The sun was setting, the pink and purple sky was magical and she breathed in how fortunate she was. Her eye condition was getting worse, but she still had sight from both eyes, although the left one was becoming more and more shadowy. She knew one day she would lose her sight completely, but for now, every chance she had, she wanted to fix each beautiful view in her mind's eye forever.

"Penny for your thoughts?" Troy stretched his hand across the table and laid it over hers. "Rose, you're such a beauty, I'm sorry, I can't help myself. I have always loved you, from that first moment in the officer's mess when I saw you reading that manual. It will never leave me."

Rose swallowed, "But it never works. I always seem to screw up and your eye wanders, and the next minute, well, I just can't do it again. Risk losing myself. Since Mum died and Dad ..." she left the thought unfinished. "Addiction. I have too many gremlins, I won't make you happy Troy. You want me to be something that I'm not. I'm not a glamour pin up girl, the way you want me to be. I like my hair short, you like it long, I want a tattoo, you hate them, even our music tastes, everything is different."

"Well Rose, if that's how you feel, so be it. I suppose I will just have to accept that I am still lucky we can work together."

His words didn't reflect the cold eyes and clenched jaw from which he delivered his empathic monologue. They ate dinner in silence and when his driver dropped her home Troy didn't get out of the car and watch her, as he usually did, until she was inside.

Rose had wanted to drink that night. She remembered the battle within herself, calling her sponsor after midnight and locking herself in the bathroom. When she had gone into the office the next day Troy had had her desk moved into a different office at the opposite end of the corridor. Over the next few weeks Troy sent her files with names she didn't recognise to set up accounts for; he kept their relationship professional and they rarely met face to face alone. It was the week before Christmas when the police came to arrest her and she was charged with fraud and embezzlement of funds. Rose would never forget the faces of the other staff as the police took her away in handcuffs. Troy was not in the office, he had flown to Belgium on business. The next time she saw him was at court. He had written, via her solicitor, offering forgiveness and suggesting mitigating circumstances; that if it were left up to him he would not press charges, but his hands were tied.

Rose served three years of a five year sentence. There had been a collective gasp when the judge announced his decision. He had taken into account Rose's history and former criminal charges related to her addiction. What baffled him the most was her betrayal of an upstanding member of the community, someone who had helped and supported her time after time. She had repaid that person with a deliberate and carefully planned scheme to steal money and his reputation from him. It was, in the judge's words, a heinous crime that must be punished to the full letter of the law.

By the time Rose came out of prison she was a changed woman. She had developed competencies she had never thought she would need. But the survival skills and the discipline she had learned in the RAF stood her in good stead and she was determined never to rely on anyone ever again. She would define what happened next, not drink or drugs or a man, or even an eye condition that had robbed her of her original dream.

Chapter Seven

December 27th

Rose fell asleep reflecting on the memories of what had gone before. When she woke up Rob had gone. He had left a note on the kitchen table

"I'm sorry, I think this is for the best. Please take care. Love Rob."

Rose didn't have time to think about anything else before her phone started ringing. "Hello."

"Rose, DI Chatterton, we need to talk to you again. Can you come here? I have a few questions and I can send a car for you."

"Do I have a choice?"

"You're not being arrested if that's what you mean, so yes, you have a choice, but I think it would be in your best interests to speak to me, don't you?"

"Sure, sorry, I've just … It doesn't matter, I'll make my own way, but I need to shower and dress first. See you in an hour."

The DI was accompanied by a younger officer when he came into the interview room. He looked tired, Rose thought, his normally tidy appearance was somewhat awry and there was a grease spot on his tie. He ran his hands over his thin greying hair.

"So, Rose, you've been asking questions I hear."

Rose looked down, "Do you mean the hospital?"

"Yes, I do Rose. You were seen by at least two witnesses who said you were acting strangely, asking for information that was none of your business. Pretending to be Doctor Reynolds' niece."

Rose flushed at being caught out in the lie. "Yes, yes I did. I wanted to know why he died. What you suspected had happened, or what you knew."

"Why?"

"Because it seemed odd that he died at the hospital, and you said as much to me when you came to the flat, that something was off. So I put it all together, with Bakti and Sally. And then there's the graffiti all over the shop, talking about drugs."

"Well Rose, what can you tell me about drugs?"

"Nothing, look I've been clean since I came out."

"Really, not a little bit of dope or alcohol has passed your lips recently?"

Rose flushed. "I had a minor relapse, panic attack." There was no point in denying it. The DI clearly knew.

"And you still insist that you didn't know Doctor Reynolds before the day he bought muffins."

"Never seen him before, or if he had been in the shop I didn't remember him."

"But your friend knows him." The DI put a photograph of Rob talking to someone in front of her on the table. She couldn't see the face of the person Rob was talking to, but from the back it could have been Doctor Reynolds.

"I didn't know they knew each other. I swear."

"Like you swore you were innocent when you were charged with stealing from your employer?"

Rose shook her head, ignoring the jibe. Why had Rob lied to her about knowing Dr Reynolds? The photograph had been taken on Morrison, near Sally's flat.

"Where did you get this, when was it taken?" Rose asked.

It was the DI's turn to ignore what was said. "And what about him? Who is he?" he said as he put another photograph on the table.

The new picture showed Rob talking to a man. They were both in profile, the man was dressed completely in black. The hood of jacket was mostly covering his face. He was carrying a gym bag.

"This must be who Teresa saw, I don't know who he is, well not from the way the picture has been taken anyway."

"Are you sure, take a good look."

Rose peered down at the photograph then shook her head "Sorry, I don't know."

"He's your delivery driver Rose."

Rose leaned her head down again, to study the picture more closely. "Even though you've told me I would never have guessed that, this man is so slim, Gary is, well he's the same height, but he's plumper. Rob told me Gary was a bad lot."

"When did Rob tell you that?"

"Yesterday after he had been trying to find out what happened to Bakti, who the undercover cop was. He had been talking to a woman, I don't know who she was."

"What undercover cop?"

"I don't know. Rob told me yesterday when he got back. He had been beaten up."

"But not badly, beaten up but not badly?"

"What do you mean?"

"Oh come off it. Do you really think the gullible act is going to work again? It didn't work the last time did it?"

"I'm not putting on an act, and how do you know he was beaten up if there's no undercover cop? Look I have notes at home, I can show you what I showed Rob. I talked to two students, one of them found Bakti, Rob was with me, they can tell you what we talked about. Please, I haven't done anything wrong."

"Have I accused you of doing anything wrong, have you been charged with anything?" The DI's eyes darted back and forth as he spoke to her.

"Well no, but you're insinuating ..."

"Insinuating exactly what Rose, that you have been asking questions? Well you admitted to that. You brought other things into the conversation, an undercover cop for example. Isn't that right?" He turned to his colleague who nodded.

"Exactly sir."

Rose looked down and started to fiddle with her hands. "Can I have some water please?"

"Yes, help yourself." He pushed the plastic jug and cups towards her. The water was warm, like the room. "How did you know which student had found Bakti?"

"I didn't, Rob told me." Rose paused, frowning, how had Rob known? "Do you want to see the notes? I don't know what else to tell you. I really didn't recognise Gary from this photograph, I didn't know Rob knew or had met Doctor Reynolds and as for Rob being beaten up, I had no reason to doubt what he told me."

The DI nodded. "Fair enough Rose. Yes I would like to see your notes and I would like a promise from you."

"Yes, what's that?"

"You will stay out of police business and not go about asking questions."

Rose nodded. "OK., can I go?"

"I'll have someone drive you home, you can give them whatever notes you have."

"Wait, there is something else."

"What is that Rose?"

"Someone broke into the flat. I have a system, in case anyone ever did break in I mean." Rose described finding the pink paper and exploring the flat afterwards. "There was nothing out of place or taken that I could see."

"Well it might be nothing, but I'll have the officer who takes you back to have a look. We can dust the door for fingerprints, although I doubt we'll find any, if what you say happened, sounds like the person was very careful."

"And the shop, can I have the graffiti removed? I'm due to re-open on January 4th. I'd like the place cleaned up."

"Well good luck finding someone to do that before then, but we have no need for you to retain what's been written. It's all been photographed and documented."

"Thanks." Rose breathed a sigh of relief. If she could get the shop open and start baking again she knew she would be fine. What on earth had she been thinking, trying to solve murders, it was too ridiculous. Yet the question about how the DI knew Rob had been attacked , why they had photographs of Rob and how he knew about the students bothered her. What if the police had been following Rob all this time? Both Trixie and Tony had warned her about Rob, but she hadn't wanted to listen. Well she was done with him now. She pulled out her phone and deleted the number she had for him and then blocked it. She knew he could still contact her but the finality of the little red sign with a line through it gave her satisfaction. At least she wasn't just rolling over.

The police officer who drove her home was a young woman. She reminded Rose of herself when she too had worn a uniform, how proud of herself she had been. She had passed the exams and qualified as a pilot, top of her group. Rose recalled her mother's face at the ceremony, beaming from ear to ear as she watched her daughter take her place on the podium. Rose's father hadn't come, but her grandparents had. Jeannie's death had devastated them but they stayed in contact with Rose until she went to prison. After that they cut her off. They had liked Troy, appreciated what he had done for Rose putting her through rehab. They made it plain they were on his side, how could she have treated him like that, let the memory of her mother down?

"Shall I bring the papers down?" Rose asked the police woman as she parked outside the flat.

"No, I'll come up. The DI asked me to take a look at the door, in case there is anything obvious about whoever broke in."

"Right" said Rose unlocking the front door, "Well you can see here it needs a key to enter, no sign of force."

"Yes, but someone could have buzzed them in, or they could have waited until someone left the building. It's your door that I want to check."

Rose felt put out by the curt response from the younger woman. "I know. We have a rule here, no one buzzes anyone in who they don't know."

The policewoman's face told Rose what she thought about her and it wasn't a look of respect. Rose wanted to yell at her, I was like you once, you smug little bitch. But what good would that do except confirm what the woman already thought of her.

The door had no signs of any intruder as Rose knew full well. But the officer did a thorough job of checking. "Where did the paper land?" She asked.

"Here, like this one." Rose held up the folded paper from the mat she had left on top of the door before she left. "The paper is the only clue that someone else was here that day." Unless Rob had been lying about that too Rose wondered, but she kept the thought to herself.

"And nothing else was moved, nothing is missing?"

"Nothing, I'm very organised as you can see. She waved her arm around the living room. Apart from the tree, there was no clutter anywhere. The pile of paperwork on the desk was stacked neatly, as were the lists Rose had pinned up on the wall.

"What's all that?"

"It's what Rob and I were doing together. Here, here are all the notes, I'll give you the lists too." Rose unpinned the lists from the wall and clipped them together. "I'm sure the DI already knows all of this."

The look the officer gave Rose said it all. Obviously.

As soon as the policewoman left, Rose set to work making another list of all the things she needed to do before re-opening, but her concentration was shot. The question about who and why had taken the photographs of Rob and Dr Reynolds and the man in black and how the DI knew about the beating and what else had Rob lied about, played on her mind, so she wrote it all out again. This time trying to separate what she knew to be facts from what Rob had told her. She made a mind map, the way her counsellor had shown her. It worked, by the time she had written everything down she felt calmer. Rose pinned the map on the wall then set to work trying to find someone who could get her shop ready for opening on the 4th. She had recipes to develop, everyone would be focusing on their health, losing weight and reducing sugar after Christmas, it was the time for dark berries, nuts and fibre.

.oOo.

"Same colours hen?" The painter she had contacted had been more than happy to come out. "Stir crazy with everyone at home." He told her cheerfully as he wrote out the materials he needed and gave her a quote for the clean-up.

"You know I think it's time for a change. Let's go bold, red for the main and blue trim. RAF colours. It means the inside will need doing as well. I'd like to contrast it. Crisp white with a lighter blue, like sky for the walls and yellow for the front of the counter. Is that all possible, I'll need it all dry and customer ready by the 4th?"

"If two of us get cracking, yes, we can do that. It'll be more than I've just quoted though."

"OK, so long as you're really sure you can do it."

"No bother at all. Glad of the money. Christmas is expensive when you've got kids."

"I expect it is. I'll make them some muffins. I'll be working in the back kitchen while you are painting, getting the new recipes ready, you can be my taste testers." Rose felt her spirits lightened by the planned makeover of her shop and the recipe ideas, she just hoped the insurance would contribute something to the exterior work, otherwise she'd have to dip deeper than she wanted into the savings she had managed to put by.

The next two days passed by in a flash as the painters started their work and Rose shopped for what she needed. The painters had left and Rose was just closing up when Teresa and Andrea came over.

"Looks good Rose" said Teresa pointing to the red paint work. "It's bold."

"Yeah, like me," Rose laughed. "How are you both, feeling better? Any more news about Bakti?"

"No, his room is still closed off but the police haven't been around for the last few days."

"Do you know where Rob is?" Andrea asked.

"No, and I doubt he'll be around here anytime soon. Why are you looking for him?" The girls exchanged glances. "Look, you're better off not knowing Rob, believe me, and I've known him for years. Don't trust him."

"OK Rose, thanks." They turned to walk away.

"Were you, were you buying from him?"

Teresa looked down. "He, well someone said he was OK, to buy from I mean. Do you know anyone else?"

Rose shook her head, "Look, after what happened to Bakti, maybe you two should ... well, I don't know. Just drink? Not that I'm a great fan of that either."

"We don't have a problem just, well we're young, you know."

"Yeah, I know. So be careful. Here, try one of these, let me know what you think."

Rose took two muffins out of the box she was carrying. They were still warm, the mixed cherry and blackberry filling oozing from the top under almond flakes.

Andrea took a bite and gave Rose a thumbs up. "Delicious Rose, thank you. When are you opening again?"

"In a week, 4th January. Take care you two."

Rose walked further up Morrison towards the crescent where Tony and Babs lived. Babs had come out of hospital that morning and she had made muffins for them. She planned to take the rest to the homeless shelter.

The shelter had been thrilled with her donation and she had spent time having a coffee and catching up with the coordinator. There had been a lot of bad stuff going around, and two of the regulars were in hospital.

"How's Trixie doing? I'm so glad she's not still here."

"Yeah, me too. She's great, went home to see her parents, she should be back around the 2nd. I told her to call me if she needed to talk, or things went wrong, but no news so far. So, it seems like it's gone well."

"Good for her and for you too Rose. Offering her that job, it made the world of difference."

"It's a good programme and she's a good worker, I don't put up with any nonsense."

The coordinator smiled, "I heard."

It was after 9pm by the time Rose got home, she was exhausted but she knew she wouldn't be able to settle. She had a plan for the interior, once the walls were painted. She would keep the glamour girls but she wanted to add old photographs of planes and women pilots, a nod to her past, before things had gone sideways. She remembered a set of black and white photographs of herself and another female pilot in uniform standing by one of the planes. They had been taken for a recruitment ad. That would work, she thought.

Rose knelt down by the ottoman. She hadn't opened it for a while. The memories it contained made her sad, but now she was ready to face them. She had forgotten how many photographs there were as she looked at each one carefully, remembering names and faces of the men and women she had trained with and those who had trained her. She had returned her uniform, but she still had the cap, it was wrapped in brown paper. She put it on and looked at herself in the dresser mirror.

Did she look so very different? Her hair was as short as it had been when she was recruited, the only difference between then and now were the lines that appeared when she smiled and the nose piercing, a small diamond she had had done to celebrate five years of sobriety. She turned to sit back down and stumbled, kicking over the pile of photographs, sending them scuttling in all directions. She reached under the ottoman to retrieve some of the photographs, but something sharp scraped the top of her hand. She lifted the corner of the wooden box and dropped it again. What the hell? Rose grabbed the rest of the contents from inside the box and turned it over to find twenty four tiny bags of white pills staring back at her.

Chapter Eight

December 30th

"Do you think this is your friend Rob's handiwork?" asked the DI? One of the officers carefully untaped the bags and placed them in a container. Another officer recorded the number of bags and their contents.

"I have no idea, but I can't imagine it was, he had no money the night came here, I washed his clothes, the only thing he had on him was his mobile phone. There was no way he could have hidden this lot when he came upstairs, his hands were full of my shopping. And he wouldn't have spent any time in my bedroom without me knowing."

"So what's your explanation then Rose? How do you happen to have so much morphine in your flat?"

"I've told you, I don't know, I can't explain it, except perhaps it was the intruder."

"The intruder who didn't take anything, left you a stash of street drugs worth several thousand pounds?"

Rose put out her hands, "I really really don't know. I haven't been near the ottoman for at least a year. And when I clean, it just gets moved, I had no reason to look underneath it.

"Well it can't have been there for too long. That tape, the way you said it caught your hand, it wouldn't have lasted, it was already beginning to turn up at the edges, so I'm guessing they wanted you to find it, whoever left it there."

"Right, or they hoped you would."

"What do you mean?"

"I've been thinking about the intruder, surely they would have seen the paper I left fall from the door. It's obvious really, especially to someone trying to be so careful. Perhaps they actually wanted me to know they had been here and expected me to call you immediately so when you searched the place you would find all this?"

The DI looked carefully at Rose. She had a sharp mind, she wasn't the sum total of the police reports, but was she too sharp. What was her role in all this? Her suggestion didn't sit well with him, it didn't fit whatever was going on. He had spotted the map on the wall in her living room as soon as he entered. Why hadn't she done as she had promised and let it all go? She was still thinking about things, trying to put the pieces together. How did she really know there was a cop working undercover? Lucky they had pulled him out, there had been too many leaks. But it was where those leaks were coming from that worried him. There were at least two paramedics who had gone rogue, the last thing he needed to find was that a member of his own team was working against him.

"I thought you and I had an agreement." The DI pointed to the map.

"We do, I just needed to clear my head. Since then I've been concentrating on getting the shop ready, but now this has happened."

"Why did you wait until this morning to call it in?"

"Because I was a mess. I wanted to ... well I wanted to drink. I knew calling you lot would prevent that, but I needed to fight it myself. So that I knew I could. If you had come over, the need, well it might still be there."

"I see."

"Do you though? Really, do you have any idea what it's like? Maybe that's why they did this, to send me off the rails again. Well, when you find them, if you find them, you can tell them it didn't work."

"Alright Rose, calm down, you've made your point. Is there anyone you can stay with, who can support you I mean. Family, friends?"

"No, Rob was my so-called friend, and none of my family speak to me. My father since my mother died and my grandparents since I went to prison."

"I'm sorry to hear that. But your mother's death, it had nothing to do with you. It was a fall."

"You are well informed. Yes, it was a fall, but my father never got over it. I've tried to reach out but he doesn't respond, other than a couple of letters. He hates me."

"Where were you when she died?

"I was with Rob. I had just left my boyfriend."

"The one who you stole from, weren't you engaged?"

"Yes, and I didn't steal from him. Anyway, that was later, after the second time in rehab, we weren't engaged then."

"Sounds complicated," said the DI.

"It was," said Rose, biting her lip.

"We're all done here sir." An officer carrying the box of drugs came through to the living room. "There doesn't appear to be anything else anywhere."

"Thank you."

Rose looked about her space, they had done a thorough job, opened every drawer, looked in and under every stick of furniture, inside the cushions, but it had all been put back apart from her bed, which had been stripped.

"Sorry about the bed, it's just routine."

"Yes, I know. It's alright, it needed changed anyway. At least I know the place is not hiding any more nasty secrets. I don't think I'm going to be baking today."

"Right, well I'll be off too. We're going to keep an eye out, it won't be much, just a drive by every hour or so, and the shop. Are you going to be alright?"

The DI's voice had changed, gone was the curt tone, he almost sounded as if he gave a damn, Rose thought. "I'll be fine."

Once everyone had gone she decided to clean everything, the flat felt contaminated, dirty. She tackled the tree first. Seeing the police rifle through the decorations, turning the pot over had sullied any pleasure she might have had from looking at it now. She took the potted tree downstairs and placed it in the little shared garden at the back of the flat. Maybe the tree would survive, be able to come back inside for next Christmas if she was still there. Still there? Why had that thought crept into her mind? Where else would she go?

Her father still lived just outside Bristol where she had grown up and her grandparents lived in Inverness. Neither place had any appeal or draw. She wouldn't be welcome, even for a brief visit. Edinburgh had been her home since she left prison; as far as she knew Troy was still in Glasgow and even though it was a big enough city for the both of them to live in and be apart, she didn't have any yearnings to go back there. She had grown to love Edinburgh, apart from the climate, it was perfect. No, she wasn't going anywhere, Rose was sure of that.

She remade the bed and tempted as she was to lie in it, have a pyjama day, she decided to get a grip on herself. She wrapped the photographs she had selected for framing and brushed her hair. The shops would be closed for two days after tomorrow, and there was still a lot to be done. Trixie was coming back on the 2nd, Rose wanted to be finished by then so they could both concentrate on the batters and prepare everything ready for the 4th.

The painters had finished the outside, they were putting the finishing touches on the interior trim when she arrived with the photographs and a new set of frames. "Happy with it?" The painter called down from the top of his ladder.

Rose looked around, "Yes, it looks great. The outside, it's so different, sharp, and this blue with the white and yellow, it makes the place bigger somehow."

"It's still cosy though. My kids loved those muffins you sent home by the way. My wife said she'll do you a review on Trip Advisor too."

"Thanks, that's really kind of her, it all helps."

"You know, in case this happens again, the graffiti I mean, have you thought about getting one of them cameras? My pal fits them, they're not all that dear."

Rose thought for a second, "No, I haven't but maybe that's not a bad idea. Could he fit one up at my home too?"

"Oh you don't need him for that, look at this."

The painter climbed down from the ladder and showed her his phone. She could see a living room, there was a cat sitting in a basket, washing itself."

"You can get one online, set it up and presto, you can watch your home through your phone."

"Right, thanks. But give me your friend's number, I'll call him about putting a camera outside here."

The bell rang as the shop door opened. "Wha's been going oan, why all the changes?"

"Trixie, you're back early. Good to see you. Yes, a fresh start for the New Year." Rose decided, in the moment, against letting Trixie know about the graffiti. She looked at the painter, her eyes flashed, communicating, don't say anything.

"Cool, although, sae different from before." Trixie picked up one of the pictures of Rose in her uniform. "Is that yersel?"

"Yes. I'm going to hang them here. Let me just finish up and we can make some tea, you can tell me how come you are back and about your Christmas."

Trixie wrinkled her nose. "I'll put the kettle oan, aye?" And disappeared into the back.

The painter tapped his nose. "I won't say, but she'll find out."

"Yes, I know, I don't want her to worry though. And she's back early. I hope nothing went wrong."

"Christmas, something's bound to happen. I'll come back tomorrow, to finish up the trim outside. I should be done by the middle of the day. I've texted you my pal's number, but it's probably going to be after Hogmanay before he's around."

The painter had already left by the time Trixie came back with two mugs of hot tea.

"Come oan Rose, wha's really been happ'ning, ye didnae hae ony plans tae change the paint colours after that survey."

Rose studied the girl, she looked tired, ashen. From her face and the way she was dressed she didn't resemble someone returning from an overindulged family festival. "It's a bit of a story, I will tell you, but you tell me first. Why did you come back?"

"Better crack here, on Hogmanay."

"Oh come on."

"Well, it will be. Och, they were fine, but I'm nae a wean noo. They had a stocking fer me."

"Too much?"

Trixie nodded, "Ay, I couldnae deal wi' it all. I said you needed me tae get the shop ready. I wasnae wrong it seems. Sae tell."

Rose bit her lip. She wasn't sure where to start, she wasn't really sure how fragile Trixie was, she was good at hiding behind banter. But the painter was right she would find out, and it would be better coming from Rose. She told her about the graffiti, that Doctor Reynolds had died in the hospital and that Rob was gone. However, she didn't tell Trixie about the morphine at her flat."

Trixie pushed her about Rob, how did Rose know, could she be sure he was gone?

"We had a row, look I know you had no time for him, but we went back years and he was there for me at one time. I thought I could do the same for him, when he was down on his luck. But it didn't work out, so he split."

"He was a two-faced monster Rose, I'm glad ye sent him pack'ng, but …"

"But what?"

Trixie looked worried, she was staring at her tea, trying to figure out how to say what was on her mind. "He's couch surfing with a so-called friend, she's relapsed. He's still in Edinburgh. I've warned her, but she, weell she's a bit like you about Rob, only wants tae see the good in him."

"Well, I doubt he'll come around here, we have another problem though. Gary."

"Gary?"

"Yes, he seems to have disappeared too. Did you know he knew Rob? We'll need somebody else if we can't manage the deliveries."

"I didnae ken he knew Rob, I liked him."

"So did I."

The two women sat in silence, pondering what had been left unsaid and the unusual circumstance of their relationship. Employer, trainee, mentor, and friend. Although the latter was still developing, Rose was carefully keeping herself back from getting too fond of Trixie, she had learned the hard way when it all came to a head with Sally and she had had to let her go.

"Shall we hang these then?" Trixie pointed to the photographs.

"Don't you want to stay on holiday, you're not due to work until the 2nd."

"I'm volunteering, hanging pictures is always better with two, to make sure everything is lined up."

"Thank you, Trixie, in that case I'll treat you to a take-away supper. Fish and chips?"

Rose locked the shop. Trixie had already left and Morrison Street was deserted. That quiet period between Christmas and Hogmanay when everyone is getting ready to welcome in the New Year. Rose wished she could magic away the Old, it was almost seven years since Troy had set the trap for her, but after the recent deaths, finding the morphine, Rob and Gary's betrayal it felt like yesterday. Despite her promise to the DI, Rose knew she couldn't stop trying to figure things out. She needed to know who was behind whatever was going on.

Chapter Nine

December 31st to January 1st

"Goodbye June." Rose said as she finished the call to Sally's grandmother, and reviewed the notes she had made. Rob was definitely in the clear as far as June knew, Sally had rowed with him. Like Rose, June had been shocked by her granddaughter's relapse. Sally had been committed to a new life, being a mother and she had enrolled in college. It turned out that Sally did know Dr Reynolds though. June didn't know how they had met, or why Sally had changed doctors. Dr Reynolds had arrived at the flat the day Sally died, when June was dropping off some lunch.

Rose unpinned the map she had made, and connected Reynolds to Sally twice, the first time on the day she died and the second on the night he was run over, when he was supposedly on his way to see Babs and Tony. Sally would have been dead for three months by then, what was he up to? She put a line from Reynolds to Rob and from Rob to Gary. Then she wrote a question mark and connected it to

Gary. Who was this and why had her shop come to their attention? There were so many small shops with kitchens around that were up for sale or to rent. Why was her property so significant suddenly?

Rose called Tony to find out how Babs was doing and to wish them both a Happy New Year. "Why don't you come over Rose, we probably won't make it to midnight, but we could toast with a wee dram together, what do you say?"

Rose hesitated, she had an ulterior motive for calling, maybe it would be better to see what Tony knew or didn't know about Dr Reynolds face to face. " Sure Tony, I have a non-alcoholic drink I can bring."

"Oh we have lots of exotic non-alcohol libation, Babs can't take alcohol because of her meds. See you around seven."

Rose put the map back on the wall and studied her handiwork. She sent a text, it was a long shot, but this was someone with connections, though not the sort of connections Rose wanted to have any longer. The text back suggested a meeting the following day in Glasgow.

Tony and Babs' flat was suitably festive when Rose arrived, the tree was magnificent and the walls were adorned with ribbon and cards. Tony had put out a meze of Mediterranean food.

Babs was sitting on the sofa, her legs up under a cotton rug. She was wearing makeup, her short blonde bob looked newly cut and she looked more relaxed than she had in a long time. The cancer drugs had apparently not affected Babs hair. Usually, Babs and Tony were both easy to talk to but tonight Rose found the conversation stilted. It was

Tony who eventually broached the subject that Rose wanted to ask him about.

"Rose, did you know Dr Reynolds knew Sally and Rob?"

"I only just found out Sally knew him when June and I talked today. The police have a photograph of Rob talking to someone that looks like Dr Reynolds. How did you know?"

"From the police." Tony's words were cautious, "There's something else, about Dr Reynolds I mean."

"Show her," Babs urged Tony.

"Show me what?"

Tony unfolded an envelope. He pulled out a stack of prescriptions all signed by Dr Reynolds, but there was nothing written on them.

"Where did you find this?"

"It was under Babs bed, I found it two days before Dr Reynolds died. It couldn't have been there for long, I clean once a week, I didn't think anything of it, I just assumed he kept them already signed as a backup. I was going to give it back to him when he came over, but then he died."

"You didn't tell the police?"

"No, I don't know why. It seems silly now, but I didn't want to get him into trouble, after he was dead. We really liked him and we thought the signed prescriptions, if anyone found out, could tarnish his reputation. Then when they asked about Rob, well we got to wondering."

"I have a feeling he was definitely not just the kind old man you both thought."

Tony nodded. "Maybe."

"I think you should let the DI know about them. Was there anything else that happened that you didn't think was odd at the time?"

"Well, it was about you actually," Babs said. "When we told him about your shop and how much we loved what you made he asked a lot of questions. They seemed innocent enough at the time, but now I realise he wanted to know quite a lot about you. How well we knew you. He told us …" Babs paused.

"What did he say?"

"He told us that you had been in prison."

"How on earth did he know? I am sure I have never met him before the day he came into the shop. Was he surprised that you already knew and still liked me?" Rose smiled.

"Och, he looked quite put out that his news was not big news to us. But Rose, any of us can make a bad decision and that's what we told him." Tony's kind face smiled warmly at her.

"You'll never know how much your acceptance has meant to me. Well you both know the whole sorry story. Let's hope the police find out what really happened to Sally the Doctor and Bakti. Cheers, here's to a New Year without Murder, let Morrison get back to normal."

"Slàinte Mhath" Tony and Babs said together as they all raised their glasses.

"And to our son," said Babs.

"To Patrick," said Rose and Tony, toasting for the second time and clinking glasses.

She wondered why Patrick had taken off, left such lovely parents. Of course, teenage children often found it hard to reconnect with their family. But after all this time, why hadn't he got in touch? It was heart-breaking to see Babs' face as they toasted her son.

It was just after nine thirty when Rose left. She felt wobbly as the air hit her face, Morrison was busy as revellers headed into the West End towards the castle for the Hogmanay street parties. She didn't see the shadow of the van pulling up behind her. She heard the van door open and turned. A man dressed in black with a balaclava ran at her. Too late, Rose put her arms up to defend herself.

.oOo.

When Rose came to, she was bound and gagged, she could feel the vibration of the vehicle as it bumped along, it didn't feel like a road, more like a track. How long had she been out? There was no light coming from the back door windows to where she was laying. Her head was throbbing and she was freezing cold. Whoever had grabbed her had removed her jacket, socks and shoes. She tried to picture the man she had seen, but it was useless, he was dressed in black but she didn't think it could have been Gary, he wouldn't have been strong enough to tackle her. The way he had avoided her lunge at him, he must have been well trained. Cursing her bad eye she tried to focus on what she could see, but it wasn't much. A transit van with nothing else in it. She was tethered to stop her sliding about, or kicking her way through the back doors, if only she had the strength. The rope was tight and she couldn't turn to see the driver and whoever had hit her. A few minutes later the van stopped, the vehicle shook as both the front doors slammed shut. She could hear raised voices, two men and a woman, they were arguing. Rose listened carefully, trying to make out what they were saying, who had kidnapped her. But none of the voices were familiar, the two men were Scottish the woman sounded like she was from somewhere in the South of England..

One of the back doors of the van opened and someone shone a torch in her face, the blinding light prevented her from seeing who it was. Then her face was covered by a blanket of some sort as her captors untethered her and pulled her out of the van. Rose willed herself to fight, move her body, but it was useless. Whoever had tied her up knew what they were doing and she was still muzzy from the blow to her head. She felt the needle jag into her arm almost as soon as her body touched the rough cold surface of the stone floor.

The last thing she remembered was hearing one of the men say, "You'd better get going," before she fell into unconsciousness once more.

.oOo.

"Miss McLaren, are ye alright hen?" It was the elderly voice of her downstairs neighbour.

Rose opened her eyes, she was lying on the pavement, against the steps outside her apartment. It was dark, raining, she had no idea whether it was night or early morning. "What time is it?" Her voice croaked, her face muscles were aching and her mouth was dry.

"Around five o'clock, I was just closing the curtains when I looked out and saw you, did you fall?"

"Umm yes, I must have. I'm all right." Rose moved her body, she could walk, just.

"Where is your coat, your shoes, maybe you had a too good Hogmanay, you were all having quite the party?"

Rose shook her head, trying to remember. She had been at Tony's, but then where, what party? "I'm sorry, I don't remember. , I'll go in, but my key?"

The neighbour tutted, the smell of alcohol coming from Rose's body told her all she needed to know. "Well, maybe you left it open, there was quite the noise when you and your guests left."

"Guests?"

"Aye, a young couple and a friend, I didnae see you leave wi them though, just after the bells. I was standing at the window to welcome in the new year."

Rose had a flash of memory, a white van. But why was she here, on the street outside, who were the guests? "Did you see what they looked like?"

"It was too dark, they looked merry enough though."

"Thanks."

"Are ye sure you're alright, will ye manage?"

"Yes, thank you. Sorry I've been a bother." Rose followed the woman through the front door and made her way upstairs. Every movement hurt, she felt like she had done ten rounds in a boxing ring. When she got to the landing she saw her front door was indeed open. There were party poppers, and streamers laying on the mat. The living room was a mess, as if several people had been over. Cans and bottles and glasses, remnants of crisps and snacks were strewn everywhere.

"Well staged," muttered Rose walking to her bedroom. She stopped. There was a half-dressed figure lying on his side on top of her bed.

Rose picked up a bottle from the table and walked slowly over to the bed, she had no idea who it was, he was about the same age as her, fit, blonde. She moved closer and was about to speak when she realised he wasn't breathing. She backed away and stumbled. What the hell was happening? Murders, morphine and now another dead body. A noise from the vestibule startled her and she stood up, she was still holding the bottle.

"Rose! Thank goodness." It was Rob.

"What are you doing here?"

"I called but you didn't answer, the old woman downstairs, she let me in, told me you had had an accident."

"She wouldn't have let you in Rob, she doesn't know you."

Rob swallowed. "Yes, she does know me, she's seen me coming in and out with you."

Rose heard another set of footsteps. "Who is that?"

"It's me Rose," said Trixie. "What the hell?" Trixie looked beyond Rose, at the body on the bed, then back to Rose. "Who is he?"

"I have no idea. We … - I need to call the police, but I don't have my phone."

"Here," Trixie handed Rose hers. "What happened to yours, to you?"

Rose held up a finger as she waited for the emergency services operator to answer. She couldn't phone the DI directly, his number along with her phone and keys was in the bag she had worn under her coat before she set off to see Tony and Babs. The only thing she could remember about last night after that was the white van.

.oOo.

The DI handed her the plastic cup of hot tea. Rose didn't know how long she had been sitting in the interview room waiting for him. She had been asked to change into a paper suit while her clothes were examined. She hadn't protested or insisted on a solicitor, what was the point? The DI read the account of the statement she had given to the officer.

"Here we are again Rose."

"Yeah, here we are again. Do you know who he is, the body on my bed?"

"Don't you know Rose?"

"You've read what I told the officer, you know I don't."

"I know what you told the officer, that's a bit different don't you think Rose?"

"Again, how can this be happening again?"

"What's happening Rose?"

"I'm being set up, framed for something I haven't done. The drugs, now this, someone dead in my flat? Why is he dead."

"Why do you think?"

"An overdose? Morphine?"

The inspector breathed in and leaned back. He studied her face. Her answer had been quick, but her expression gave nothing away. A poker face.

"Why do you think you are being framed for something Rose. I haven't cautioned you, you are not under arrest."

His words were repetitive, almost the same as the ones he had spoken last time she had sat across a table from him. Was it the same one? He was right, no one had suggested she had done anything wrong. Yet her stomach told her it was coming, that somehow everything was going to be laid at her door. What had Rob been doing at the flat? Why was Trixie with him?

"OK then, so why are you questioning me, examining my clothes?" She knew her question wasn't rational, everything that was happening was about procedure. After all, it wasn't every day that a person found a half-dressed dead body on their bed or thousands of pounds of morphine hidden under some furniture.

"Would you like a solicitor Rose?"

"Do I need one?"

The DI got up. "I'll be back shortly."

Rose stiffened and looked at the younger officer sitting on a chair near the door. He nodded to his superior as he left the room and looked down. Was he ready for another one or two hour wait, wondered Rose. But the door opened almost as soon as it had closed.

"You are free to go Rose, although we will likely need to talk again. You can change and the officer you met last time will drive you to a hotel. Your flat is still a crime scene I am afraid."

"I don't have my purse, it was in my bag, I don't know what happened to it, or my phone."

"You don't need to worry, the hotel is at our expense. The officer can bring things from your flat if you tell her what you need overnight. It's best if you stay out of sight for a couple of days, until you can return home.

"But my shop, can I go there?"

"No, we'd rather you didn't."

"Why won't you tell me what's going on. If you are protecting me from someone, who is it?"

"Who did you contact yesterday Rose?"

"What do you mean?"

"Before you went to see your friends, you contacted someone, someone from your past. Who was it?"

Rose didn't answer.

"Who did you contact?"

"I don't remember."

"I thought it was only after you left your friends you didn't remember anything, apart from a white van? We have the van on CCTV by the way."

"You do!"

"Who did you contact Rose?"

"Marion, I called Marion."

The DI nodded. "She's a big fish Rose."

"Yeah, it's been a long while."

"So why now?"

"I need her help."

"And did she?"

"What?"

"Help. "Well did she?"

"Duh, this has all happened. I'm guessing not. What do you think?"

"I think you should stop poking your nose into places that can get you into trouble."

"So you say, but all I have done is make a list, re-decorate my business and talk to friends."

"How do you know they are friends?"

Rose shook her head. "Well, Rob I don't know anymore, but Tony, and Babs are just very sweet people and Trixie is working for me."

The DI nodded. "Well there you are then. If those are the only people you have spoken to. I'll let you know when you can go back to the flat. Take care Rose."

Rose got up, she was more confused than ever, what was the DI saying, how did he know she had contacted Marion? Was he warning her that Rob wasn't a friend, the way Tony and Trixie had? Or was this about Marion?

Chapter Ten

Four years earlier

The hostel was clean enough and Rose was glad to at least have her own room after three years of sharing a tiny cubicle. This space wasn't much bigger, but it was hers. The rules weren't bad either and so long as she was back by ten, she could please herself, but she was serious, she wasn't going back to prison, ever. She looked at the various programmes on offer and kept coming back to the same idea. She wanted her own business. She had the head for it, she'd learned enough about running things efficiently from her father. But there were barriers to everything and for the business programme she needed support, a guarantor. Rose knew it was a long shot when she wrote to her father asking him if he would support her application for a grant.

The letter he sent back was crude. Once again he accused her of causing her mothers death, and made it clear this was the last letter he'd ever write to her, and that she should never write to him again. She was dead to him.

Who would buy cakes from a vulgar slattern. Take off the rose-tinted glasses. Look at yourself. You are a disgrace. A wasted offspring that should never have been born.

Rose had torn up the letter. Her fury mixed with hurt ignited her, and over the next six months she poured her energy into attaining her new dream, despite everything. No more 'no's' she had said to Marion who was also staying at the hostel on a mandatory release permit.

It was Marion who encouraged her, even helped her with the paint colours "What would a shop run by a vulgar slattern look like?" Rose had asked her.

"Oooh, now you're asking, red and black, with gold trim."

"So the opposite, if it sold cakes?"

"Fondant fancies, those sort of pastel colours."

"You're brilliant," said Rose, "I'll be an undercover vulgar slattern."

The two women laughed uproariously.

"Can I help Rose? I have money if you need it."

"Thanks, but I need to do this myself, if dad won't guarantee me, I'll find someone who will. Maybe that chaplain, he was the one who told me about this programme."

"Alright, but if you need anything, ever, get in touch. I mean it Rose."

"What are you going to do Marion?"

"Well, I'm not going back that's for sure, and I'm not going to work for anyone else either, I have a business to re-ignite Rose, only I won't be selling cake."

Rose nodded. Marion had looked after her and shown her the ropes for surviving prison. Rose hadn't realised until later just how powerful Marion was. She was safe so long as you were on the right side of her. In the end it was Marion who made sure Rose got the references and signatures she needed for her grant.

"We can still sort out that loser for you, if you change your mind," Marion told her on their last day at the hostel, as they exchanged contact information.

"I'm hoping Karma will do that somehow," said Rose. "Now I have everything in place, once I've finished the business course, to be able to look for premises and somewhere to live I'm leaving all thoughts about him behind. Getting on with my future."

"After what he did Rose, you deserve to get some justice for yourself, and I don't mean through the court."

"Yeah, I know what you mean but honestly Marion, I've learned how resentment just eats away at you. It's what took me down in the first place. I drank to get away from what I was feeling about leaving the RAF because of my eyes, about my mum, and about Troy."

"OK, but I'm there if ever you need it."

Marion, like Rose, had a soft underbelly, although she rarely showed it. Rose reminded her of her kid sister who had fallen off a horse and died. Marion had been thirteen. Her sister, eight. The tragedy had torn the family apart and at fifteen Marion left school and ended up becoming a matriarch, running the house and managing her three brothers until they were old enough to fend for themselves. She had learned early how to beat a system that is supposed to be there for the have-nots but which effectively punishes them for being too poor.

Rose left for Edinburgh the following day, to start the business course she had enrolled in, the first step in the grant programme. The bus ride from her temporary accommodation to the college should have been quick and easy, but she managed to get lost. By the time she arrived in the classroom the introductory formalities were almost finished. Rose hated being late and she felt herself flush as she entered the classroom and saw the other students looking around. She slid silently into a seat at the back and held on to her coat and bag while one of the students opposite finished introducing himself.

"Thank you Nigel, I think that's everyone, except for the young woman at the back. Can you stand up, tell us who you are, why you are taking this course?"

The teacher, Sarah Pink, was younger than Rose, attractive with shoulder length brown hair. Her smile was encouraging but it did not help settle Rose's nerves. Rose had rehearsed what she would say about herself, how to cover up the three-year gap since she had last worked, and why she had left the RAF. but looking around at the other students she couldn't remember anything, her mind was blank. What was she doing here? Rose gathered a few thoughts and stood up quickly.

"Hello, I'm Rose, I'm going to open a muffin shop," but the rest of her speech stuck in the back of her throat and she sat back down, her coat and bag clattering to the floor.

"Thank you Rose, short and sweet, hopefully you can tell us more another time."

The course was divided into three one-month modules, writing a business plan, finances and marketing. The materials were familiar to Rose, especially the finance module, she had Troy to thank for that. It was marketing, the final module she found the most challenging. Rose passed, but she wasn't used to just scraping through.

"How can I change this?" Rose approached Sarah who was clearing up the classroom, with her final results.

"You'd have to retake I am afraid Rose, but why would you bother? You have passed and from what I see you will make a success. It was really only the marketing modules that brought your scores down. You have a vision, and clearly from the baking you brought in for everyone these past three months you are exceptionally talented."

Rose looked down, "Am I though?"

"Why do you think you're not?" Sarah leaned into her and, for a moment, Rose was confused by the sudden feelings of tenderness and frisson as they stood closer together. Sarah touched her arm. It wasn't the first time she had felt this way when Sarah was close to her. There was something about Sarah that made Rose feel tender, vulnerable.

"Of course, it ... I will be fine." Rose pulled herself up straight, what was she doing? Why show anyone that she was vulnerable, she had survived too much to give anything of herself away again. Marion had shown her the importance of keeping her guard. Rose rushed out the room, she could hear Sarah calling after her but she daren't look back. Rose wanted to put as much distance between her and whatever had just happened as possible. She tore along the corridor, which was unusually quiet and was just about to push open the swing doors when she slipped, she hadn't seen the wet floor sign.

"Oops a daisy," said the tall older man walking towards her. In Hollywood terms he was a silver fox, lean, rugged with a well-cut mane of thick silver hair.

"Damn it, I didn't see the sign," Rose explained as she scrambled up.

He bent over and helped her collect the papers that had scattered from her folder. "Ah one of Miss Pink's students I see."

"Former student, I just graduated from the course."

"How did you find it?"

"It was great."

"I hear she's an excellent teacher, from some of my students."

"Oh, you teach here?" Rose was surprised, the way he was dressed, his demeanour he didn't look like a teacher. But what did she know? Did she look like an ex-con from the outside?

"Rose, are you alright, you took off so suddenly, I wanted to give you these."

It was Sarah, she was holding out a tiny box, offering it to Rose.

"What is it?"

"Ah, I think I know!" said the older man. "She's quite famous for them."

Rose took the box and opened it. Inside was a pair of earrings, tiny circles with what looked like hand painted muffins on them. They were delicate but the images were bold.

"I make them, it's a hobby," Sarah said awkwardly. Usually she picked out two or three students who, for whatever reason, had inspired her art. Sometimes it was a pin, other times earrings or even a painted rock, that could be used as a paperweight or door stop.

"Thank you."

"Tony, how are you?" said Sarah, "I hear you are planning to retire soon."

"Indeed, I think it's about time don't you my dear?"

"I think you will be missed."

Tony nodded, "Well I'll probably still teach a class at the university, Morrison is handy for our flat.

"Actually, it's rather a good thing you two met. Rose, Tony is renowned for his knowledge of Edinburgh and business premises. He has helped several of my students in the past find somewhere to rent."

Tony frowned, he looked put out by Sarah's exuberant introduction. But he recovered quickly, nodded and pulled a card from his jacket pocket. "Well, I'm not quite so well informed as Sarah suggests, but please do give me a call Rose. Let me know what you are looking for. Now if you'll excuse me."

The two women watched him walk away.

"Rose, I'm sorry about before, if I did anything to upset you." said Sarah, breaking the silence.

"No, no you didn't, I just had a wobble, my results, I was being stupid. As you say I passed and that's all I needed to do to satisfy the grant people, now I can finally get set up."

"Well, let me know when you do, I'll definitely be bobbing over to sample some of the muffins."

Rose nodded, knowing she wouldn't do that. There was too much of something going on for her in regard to Sarah that she didn't understand, or didn't want to understand. "Thanks for the earrings," she said, pocketing the small box in her jacket, wondering if she would keep them as she walked out the front doors of the college, promising herself a new life without drama.

It was August 1st, a full year after she had left prison, when Rose examined the cheque from the foundation which had awarded her the grant to open her business. It was enough to rent a shop that didn't need too much of an overhaul, buy supplies and put a deposit on a cheap flat, if such a thing existed in Edinburgh. She was tired of being in a hostel. The grant had two conditions, one was the business course she had just completed and the second was to provide satisfactory accounts and a progress report every quarter in order for the next quarter's money to be released. She didn't need to make a profit, but she did need to prove the business was sustainable in order to receive a final grant of £5,000 at the end of the first year of trading.

There was also a lot of paperwork and monthly reports to be completed and sent in. She scoured the internet, newspapers and approached various business and flat letting agencies, but everything she looked at either needed too much work done, was too expensive, or was not in an area Rose thought would work. She decided to call Tony. She knew he hadn't seemed thrilled at the prospect of helping her, but he could always say no, if he had just given her the card out of politeness.

"Yes Rose, of course I remember, and I would be happy to see what I can do. Let's meet for coffee and you can tell me exactly what you are looking for," he said when she called him.

The man Rose had met at the college and the one who turned up for their meeting were quite different. He was still charming but Rose could tell he had his business head on. He asked her a lot of questions about her background, where she came from, why she had ended up in Edinburgh. He seemed to like that she was independent, not close to a large family, and was single. When she finally shared with him that she had been in prison, hence the grant that made all this doable, he didn't state any concerns. In fact her situation seemed to spur his intention to help her. Two days later he showed her a tiny shop with a back kitchen on Morrison Street.

"I know the owner well, the size is the problem for most businesses, but it sounds as if you aren't going to be running a cafe as well."

"This is perfect. The location, the rent, everything. Just needs a coat of paint. How do I get in touch with the owner?"

"He's away a lot, abroad, lives somewhere quite remote. I can handle all that for you. I did it for the last tenant too. He also has a flat, you mentioned you needed somewhere to live. Do you want to see it?"

"Thank you, Tony. I am so glad I met you that day."

"Me too Rose, and my wife Babs would like to meet you as well. If you're free later, can we offer you some supper. Oh, and by the way, you might see me coming and going upstairs, I err manage the property for the owner, he keeps various bits and pieces up there."

Rose nodded. She couldn't believe her luck. A shop and a flat and perhaps two new friends all in one day. Sometimes the unbelievable really happened.

Chapter Eleven

January 2nd

Marion was sitting with her back to the window when Rose arrived. She finished texting and put her phone on the table, face up. "Hello kid," she said, gesturing to Rose to sit down and waving at one of the young servers. "Coffee."

"Thanks for coming over," said Rose.

Marion nodded, but her expression was far from warm and fuzzy. "Rose, for God's sake you shouldn't have sent stuff like that over text. It's deleted but, someone has got eyes on you honey."

"It's a new phone, I don't know where the other one is, my jacket and my bag were both taken off me, all I remember about that night is a white van."

" And where you were before."

"Yes, that too, I was with friends."

"Really?"

"What do you mean?"

"Someone knew you contacted me and set you up. Who else knew your plans?"

"But it was all spontaneous, the drink at Tony and Babs I mean. I wasn't planning to go out."

"Yet there was a so-called party and a dead body at your flat."

Rose nodded.

"Look, this is nuts but do you think …" Marion paused.

"It couldn't be. Not after all this time, why would he?"

"If it stinks like a fish, it usually is. I'm already on it."

Rose opened her mouth to speak, but she had no words.

"Close your mouth, you don't know what you'll catch. Look, last time he trapped you with financials, now you're doing well, maybe he isn't done having a paddy about losing you. After all you did throw a pretty big rock back at his face. That has to hurt."

"But it's been four years since then, I've been running the shop for three."

"Well if he's clear I'll know later. OK."

"You don't hang around do you?"

"Not where people I care about are concerned and Rose, I care about you. You've somehow caught the attention of some pretty nasty people, I'm trying to figure out who and why."

"You mean apart from Troy?"

Marion shrugged and pulled a face. "How's Rob?"

Marion had met Rob when she and Rose were at the hostel. He had been clean then, supporting Rose.

"He relapsed, I helped him through it, he got a gig, fell in love, then crashed again when both those things didn't work out. And now, I don't know. He came to the flat yesterday morning, when I found whoever that was on my bed. I don't know whether to trust him or not."

"He's not sharp enough for whatever's going on. He'd be a risk to anyone, I wouldn't use him. Too fragile, like you Rose."

"I'm not fragile."

"Not on the outside honey, but you're a teddy bear and you know it. The hair looks good by the way."

Rose put her hands up to feel the short cut. "Thanks, I'm starting to get little silver hairs, I keep tweezing them."

"Did Rob mention someone called Snake to you?"

Rose shook her head.

"OK. Well, he's from Glasgow, I saw him off, he was bad news. I took over what he had and last I heard he thought he could set up in Edinburgh, against some old geezer who's been running things. But it hasn't worked. If it's him I just don't know why he might have picked on you, unless it's to get at me."

"Really?"

"Nah, I don't think so, but I can't figure out who the old man is. No one seems to know, he's like invisible. You're going to have to change your coordinates by the way."

Rose looked down at her wrist. The code Marion had given her so they could stay in touch, was hidden in the tattoo. The coordinates were Marion's mother address, all she had to do was add zero's.

Marion pushed a piece of paper towards her. "Be more careful next time."

"Sorry."

"Tech is changing so fast. I keep one step ahead and so should you."

"I shouldn't have to or need to, I'm just trying to sell muffins for goodness sake."

Marion laughed. "Well there's one type of muffin you could make that would make you a small fortune. I'd back you."

"No thanks Marion."

Marion's phone pinged. She winked at Rose, put some change on the table and left without another word. Rose sat staring out of the window at the now vacant space. She had no way of getting in touch with Rob or he with her, even Trixie. She had no idea what had happened to those two after the police had taken them all down to the station. All her numbers and contacts were lost with her phone. Would Trixie have gone to the shop, looking for Rose? They were supposed to be getting everything ready for opening. But the DI had been adamant, telling her to stay away until he contacted her. Even this meeting had broken the agreement, but she trusted Marion to help her way more than she trusted DI Chatterton.

She thought back to Marion's comments about friends. The DI had said something similar, almost as if he knew something, but couldn't tell her. What was it he was trying to say?

A small van parked outside the coffee shop. It was a locksmith. "Hey," Rose called over to him as he was leaving, "Can you replace a lock for me?"

Rose went back to the hotel, the locksmith said he would get the keys to her by 4pm. It was just after 12pm.

Rose turned on the television and flicked through the channels absentmindedly. She couldn't settle. Could it be Troy be at the back of all this, but to what purpose, and why after all this time? To have her sent to prison again? Destroy her business, her reputation? Clearly she hadn't done any of the murders. She sat on the bed and started making a list on the hotel stationery, adding Troy and the name Marion had mentioned, Snake. Could he be the question mark on her mind map?. She looked at all the names again and drew lines between who, what and where were connected. Who on that list had the answer, could make the pieces of the puzzle fit together? She jumped as someone tapped on the door, it was the DI.

"Can I come in Rose?"

"Yes, give me sec." Rose checked her appearance in the mirror. She looked puffy, tired.

"Good news, you can go back home later today. Is this your bag?" He held up the soft grey shoulder bag Rose had taken with her to Tony's.

"Yes, how did you find it? Where?"

"It was handed in, sometime on New Year's day. A woman found it. It's empty I'm afraid, except for this." It was a list of recovery meetings Rose had intended to go to over the holiday.

"How did you know it was mine?"

"I didn't, it was that young officer who drove you home, remember? She spotted it when it came in. Sharp eyes that one."

"But nothing to tell you who attacked me that night?"

"No, sorry, we did check it, but just your prints." The DI looked over to the bed and spotted the list Rose had been writing out. "Really Rose?"

"Yes, I can't stop thinking about everything, the puzzle is driving me mad. Surely you understand that."

He picked up the paper and studied it carefully. "I see Troy is on here, your ex right? How come?"

"It's, well, because this is what happened before. I was trapped and suddenly my life was over. He did say something like *'it's not over between us'*, like the note that was pushed through the door."

"When did he say that?"

"When I rejected him, at the end of my sentence, he proposed. He'd even bought a ring."

"There's nothing to suggest he's involved but I'll take a look."

"This name, how do you know him?" He was pointing to Snake.

"I don't know him. He's somebody from Glasgow."

"Who now lives in Edinburgh. He's a nasty piece of work Rose. Any point me telling you to stay out of things or how you happen to have his name?"

Rose smiled. "Probably not, but if anything ... I mean, if I think of anything I will tell you. Honestly, I just want my simple life back, the one I had before Sally died. Before she was murdered. What? Why are you looking at me like that?"

The DI smiled, "Just that you don't appear to have led a very simple life."

"I know, it was supposed to be though. RAF, then NASA."

"Most people wouldn't call that simple."

"I was lucky that I even had a shot at it, and despite everything I would do it the same, if I was young again I mean. Would you? Join the police?"

"Yes, I would. A car will pick you up, is an hour enough time to get ready?"

"I'm ready now, five minutes."

"Alright then, I'll drive you."

Rose packed the jeans, sweater and nightwear the officer had brought her to change into yesterday. She looked around, usually a hotel room would have been her idea of heaven. But she couldn't wait to get home, even though she knew she was going to have a struggle with the memory of finding a dead body on her bed.

"Do you know who he was, that man on my bed?"

"Yes, but we can't release any details yet, we need to talk to the family first. I expect you'll find out tomorrow."

"On the news?"

"No Rose, I will come and tell you myself."

"OK. Is the flat still a mess?"

"I expect so, they'll have taken away what they need, but I'm sorry any of the mess left will be yours.

They drove back to her flat in silence. Rose was deep in thought. If the inspector was going to tell her personally who it was that was on her bed, that must mean something. But she hadn't recognised him, so whoever he was must be connected to someone on the list.

The flat wasn't as bad as she'd remembered. All of the bottles and cans had been removed. Her bed had once again been stripped, but this time the bedding was gone too. She took fresh linen out of the cupboard, and took it through to the living room. She wasn't ready to manage the bedroom yet, the ghost of the dead man was too close. She would sleep on the sofa bed. She called the locksmith to let him know the change of plans, arranged to meet him at the shop and then get him to change the key to the door of her flat and make a copy for the main front door, from her spare. Although that should be changed too. She would need to speak to Tony, ask him to get the building owner's permission.

Rose found a note from Trixie when she arrived at the shop. *Call me when you can, I can come over anytime.* The locksmith made quick work of the change. But when she showed him her spare for the main front door of the flat, he shook his head. "I can't cut those; you'll need a specialist and permission."

"Darn, that means I have to go back with you. OK let me make a call." Rose phoned Trixie from the landline, "Can you be here in an hour? Sorry, we'll be late getting everything ready. Is that ok?"

"Yes Rose, of course. Can Rob come too?"

"What? You've changed your tune."

"Yes, he's really upset, he stayed here last night. There's stuff he needs to tell you."

"He can come, but any confessions will have to wait until we're done with prepping for opening."

"Thanks," Rose heard Rob shouting from the background. "And I can clean too."

It was gone 9 o'clock by the time Rose was ready to call it a day. She sent Trixie home in a taxi and took Rob back to hers. Rose put a frozen pizza in the oven. She couldn't face cooking. Rob looked around.

"Do you feel safe here Rose?"

"Not really, not now, I loved this flat, maybe I will again. I don't know but I'll just have to get on with it for now, won't I? So come on, tell me how come you stayed with Trixie last night? You two were arch enemies just before Christmas."

Rob nodded, "I let her down Rose, like I've let you down and Bakti. Talked too much, behaved like an arse."

"And …," Rose threw her hands up in the air. "For God's sake Rob stop rambling feeling sorry for yourself and get to the point."

Rob swallowed. "OK. Sorry. You asked me before, if I knew Dr Reynolds. Truth is I did and I knew what he was up to. He had supplied me before, he specialised in making legal prescriptions available to the well-heeled. I worked for him for a bit, he asked me about you, it was just before Sally died. Wanted to know how close we were and how close you were to Tony and Babs. I told him, and I didn't think anything of it really, not until you told me he'd been run over.

"Was he involved in what happened to Sally?"

"I don't know, but I don't think so, I thought Gary might have been."

"Gary?"

"Yeah, it's his brother who was on your bed."

"How the hell do you know that? And why didn't you say you knew who it was when you came here yesterday?"

"I'm trying to tell you everything Rose, but it's not coming out in order. Will you just let me tell you, best I can?"

"Please do, I'm all ears and Rob, everything you tell me, I'm recording it." Rose held up her new phone.

Rob nodded. "Fair enough. I didn't know it was Gary's brother until later. And I didn't mean Gary had been responsible for Sally. Look, it's complicated, and in my own way I have been trying to protect you, except well as I said before I've made things worse, I just don't know how."

"You're not making any sense Rob. How did you know Gary?"

"I met him in the summer. I was meeting Bakti and we got chatting outside the building. He asked me if I knew where to get some gear, he said someone had pointed me out. I wasn't sure to be honest, I mean, it sounded unlikely, so I followed him. He was working for someone I had heard about, but I didn't know who they were. A guy called Snake.

"Snake!"

"Yeah, have you heard of him?"

Rose nodded. This morning, I met Marion, she mentioned him."

"Snake has been trying to get everyone working for him, including me. When I refused, I got the message that I'd be sorry. When Bakti was killed and the police hauled me in for questioning, I thought Gary must have had something to do with setting me up. He was there that day. He saw me and he knew I'd seen him. You see I knew Bakti hadn't committed suicide before we heard it on the news. I was there. That's how I knew who the students who had found him were,"

"Gary killed Bakti?"

"I wasn't sure, but now I know it wasn't him. But I was sure Bakti was killed because of me. Then when Gary started working for you I thought maybe they were coming after you too, because of me."

"Rob if you thought knowing me was the problem, why on earth did you come here? And why didn't you tell the police what you knew? And I still don't understand why Gary's brother was left dead in my bedroom and how you knew who he was."

"I'm coming to that. I was wrong about Gary. He is working for Snake, but he had nothing to do with Bakti's death. They are as confused as we are about why he was killed and who did it."

"So you two just had a cosy chat?"

"No, it was Gary that stopped the kids who had set on me. I lied about what happened, about who beat me up. I was sure I was going to be a goner, there were six of them, but when Gary turned up they ran. He had a knife. I assumed he was going to attack me but he put the knife away and we talked. He was in pretty deep with Snake, but weird things were happening. Snake had thought you were part of running a cartel here, but they couldn't figure out who you were in partnership with. So when Gary had approached me, it was because he knew I knew you and then, when you advertised for a delivery driver ..." Rob opened his hands. "I should have said something. I knew they wanted to move in and needed information to know who to take out. So, I said I'd help."

Rose stared at Rob. "I seem to be good at picking people who just want to destroy me. After Troy, you are one hell of a piece of work, Rob. A star performance. But why does Trixie trust you now if she knows all this and again, why was Gary's brother left dead on my bed?"

"I told Trixie everything. Look, whoever killed Bakti, Dr Reynolds and Gary's brother are doing this as a warning to Snake. To let him know he's not going to win. They used Gary's brother as a threat, the way they used Bakti. Gary has gone underground, I sent him a text with the picture of the dead man just before the police arrived. It was only after the police had finished asking me questions, he told me who it was."

"Your solution is way too complicated. Why not just go after Snake, you and Gary. And again, why my bed and why was I dragged off the street like that?"

"I can't figure that out Rose, it's like Sally's body, why was she left outside your shop?"

"Alright, so why did you and Trixie come here yesterday morning?"

"Looking for you. We had both had the same idea to surprise you, first footing after the bells for a toast, we met outside. Trixie was not best pleased to see me. Your neighbour was standing at her window, she was banging a pot, and some other people were leaving, we guessed they were just neighbours. I buzzed but you didn't answer so

Trixie and I left, I offered to walk her home. As we walked I dumped everything that I knew on her. She wanted to go to the police, but then I got a text from you to say Happy New Year, and to meet you here in the morning. You said you had a surprise. Look." Rob held up his phone to show Rose the text. "We decided to come over together and talk to you, see what you wanted to do."

"But how did you get in?"

"This, Rob held up a key."

"How did you get that?"

"Gary gave it to me, the day before yesterday."

"Where did he get it from?"

Rob shrugged.

"So was he the one who broke in? Left all that morphine?"

"No. It wasn't him."

"How can you be sure?"

"It's not Snake's style to lose money, leaving gear for the police to find. Gary would have known if there had been a plan like that."

"But this key, the main front door key, can't be copied. I only found that out today from the locksmith. So, whoever had it, or however Gary got it, it must have come from the owner."

"Rose, if you have money you can get whatever you want."

"True."

"Sorry Rose."

"About setting me up you mean."

"I wasn't going to do that, I was just trying to find out who and what you knew, I knew you didn't have anything to do with the cartel, but I needed Gary to persuade Snake of that. He knows you and Marion were at the hostel together."

"How did he know that?"

"I told Gary. I'm sorry. I told you I behaved like an arse."

"And so you should be, but now someone else, not Snake, is trying to frighten me and I have no idea who. It doesn't explain why Reynolds was killed though, or Sally. And ..."

"What is it?"

Rose scrambled to her feet and took the mind map off the wall and compared it to the list she had made earlier in the hotel.

"I've just remembered, Tony showed me those prescriptions you talked about. A stash of unsigned ones he found in an envelope under Babs' bed. What if Dr Reynolds hadn't left them there by accident?"

"As a safe place you mean?"

"Well, no, where he left them was too obvious. What if he was trying to involve Tony somehow?"

Rob shook his head and studied what Rose had written down. "I think you should connect Dr Reynolds to Snake."

"But I thought you said he was independent, didn't have anything to do with Snake?"

"Well as far as I knew he didn't, but maybe things changed. It would connect the murders. Look." Rob took the pen and wrote Snake at the top of the paper with lines down to all four murder victims. Under those names he wrote, Gary, Rob, Tony and Rose."

"That doesn't work as a pattern," said Rose. "Gary's brother is a blood relative, Bakti was your lover, but Doctor Reynolds and Sally, they were professional contacts. Yes, I was fond of Sally, but we weren't close. and although both of them knew Tony they weren't really significant to him."

Rob looked despondent as his eyes scanned the names. "Shall we start again?"

Rose nodded, "But not tonight. Look, I'm using the sofa bed, you're welcome to use the bed, if you feel ok about that, do you have anywhere else?"

"Well Trixie or Marion's, but she's using. I think I'd prefer to be here, and I'm fine using the bed. Thank you."

Chapter Twelve

January 3rd Part 1

Sleep evaded Rose until the early morning, it was already past 9 o'clock by the time she stumbled off the sofa bed. Rose phoned Trixie. "Hey sorry I've slept in, are you already on your way?"

"Och, nae bother. I was here early. Lucky you gave me a spare key, I told Tony the locks were changed by the way."

"Tony's there?"

"Ay, he's upstairs. He was surprised tae see me I think. He didnae realise we would be working today. He was asking after ye. He didnae ken what happened to ye, on Hogmanay."

"I'll be there as soon as I can."

Rose stared at her phone. Rose was sure the DI had said they had spoken to Tony, so why would he tell Trixie he didn't know about her being attacked and grabbed off the street after she left the flat? She dressed quickly and checked in on Rob. He was still sleeping. She left him a note and hurried over to the shop. There was a smattering of frost, but the sun was bright and the walk through the park settled her. The dreams that had disturbed her sleep had been a continuum of long dark passageways leading to locked doors. Each time she had tapped on one, she found herself at the beginning of another long passageway. Rose knew the only way she was going to be able to think properly, concentrate, was to clear her mind completely. She had learned how to do that when she learned to fly. Despite what you know, or think you know, every time you approach a plane, do it as if it was the first time. Never skip a step and don't take anything for granted, the instructor had told them. She applied the same methodology to creating recipes. Whatever worked in one batter did not apply to another. A small change, an added ingredient, meant every step had to be considered carefully. Cooking was a science, a mathematical conundrum and artistic flair all rolled into one. Surely the same principles apply to detecting and solving murders she thought as she rid her mind of the map and lists she had created. Rob was right. They needed to start again.

Trixie had sanitised and prepped everything ready for the new biscuit dough and batters they had tested yesterday.

"Good work Trixie, and thanks," Rose said as she looked over the recipes and checked off the ingredients.

"I gave Tony one of the wee samples from yesterday. He loved it."

Rose nodded. "So, what did he say when you told him what had been going on, why I had the locks changed."

Trixie put her head to one side. "Nae much, he said he hoped you were braw the noo, tae let him know if ye needed anything and if ye could gie him a key. Sorry Rose, should I no hae said?"

"It's fine, he has to have a key. I'll pop up and see him once we've got the biscuit batches in." But just as they were getting started the DI interrupted their work, he wanted to talk to Rose about the dead man on her bed.

"I went to the flat and found your friend. He told me where you were. Can we talk?"

"Sure," We can sit in the shop.

"Rob told me you already know the dead man is Gary's brother."

Rose nodded. "It was late last night when Rob told me, should I have called you?"

"No, we knew that yesterday morning, about the same time Rob found out apparently. But I am a bit surprised that you trust Rob, after everything that has happened."

"He's not a suspect though is he? I mean he's been an idiot, but he hasn't had anything to do with the murders."

"Or the break in? How come he has a key?" asked the DI.

"He got the key, yesterday from Gary."

"And you believe him?"

"Yes, look we went round in circles last night, the only solution that made sense is that someone was trying to scare Snake off, but what we couldn't figure out was why they were also trying to involve and scare me."

The DI ignored her statement. Instead he pulled a picture out of the envelope he was carrying. "Do you know who this man is?" The DI put the picture of an older man with a deep tan, lying by a pool, in front of her.

"No idea."

"Well he owns this place, and the building where you rent your flat. And several other properties around Edinburgh."

"I've never met him, Tony manages this building and my flat for him. I pay the rent to Tony, well to a company. Edinburgh Lettings Incorporated."

"What about him?" The DI handed her another photograph.

Rose stared at the picture of her ex shaking hands with the man in the previous image. They were both wearing suits and it looked like they were in the conference area of the hotel Troy used for meetings in Glasgow.

"Troy!"

"Bit of a coincidence, or maybe nothing at all."

"Where did you get this?"

"We were searching for this man," he pointed to the first picture. "It was taken last year. August 30th to be precise. Did Troy contact you, or did Tony mention the building owner was in town?"

"No. In fact, last August, Tony went to visit the owner, or so he told me. To the Seychelles, with Babs. It was just before she was diagnosed with cancer. And I haven't seen or heard from Troy since that day in the prison, when I rejected his proposal. What does he have to do with this?"

"Nothing, there's no evidence to suggest he does. We've not spoken to him of course, and from looking at what's available publicly, he hasn't even been to

Edinburgh. He flies in and out of Glasgow and any trips he takes seem to be to Europe."

"You can find that all out without asking him?"

"It's amazing what people share on social media, even business social media."

"When you were with him, did he ever mention his family?"

"No, he had loads of friends, he always said they were his family. I don't even know the names of his parents or grandparents. He didn't have any pictures of them and, well the one time I did ask, it was early on in our relationship, he got really upset - angry even. So I didn't bother after that."

"And your parents, did he meet them? Was that all fine?"

"Yes, I mean, it was odd how he behaved sometimes, almost as if he was jealous of me and my mum. How close we were. We visited when we could, Bristol and Glasgow are not exactly next door. I spoke to mum on the phone nearly every day and sometimes he got annoyed about that."

The bell of the door jingled as it opened. It was Tony. Rose looked up as Tony approached the table. He glanced down at the pictures the DI had been showing Rose.

"I won't be a minute Tony, I'm just talking to the Inspector."

"Yes, sorry to disturb, I popped in for the key, Rose, I'm all finished upstairs and I need to get back to Babs." Tony put his hand out to the DI. "Nice to see you again. I hope you get all this business sorted out. Poor Rose, she must have had quite a scare," but Tony wasn't looking at DI Chatterton as he spoke, his face was fixed firmly on the photographs.

Rose frowned, why had Tony told Trixie he didn't know what had happened if he had met with the DI? Of course she knew they would have met before because of Doctor Reynolds, but there was something off, why mention she would have been scared to the inspector if they hadn't discussed it? He could have called her, asked her to drop the key off at the flat?

"Let me get you the key, Tony." Rose went to the back where Trixie was baking the first batch of biscuits.

"Did you hear?" she mouthed at Rose, putting her fingers over her lips to let Trixie know to respond silently. Trixie nodded.

Rose gave Tony the key and said, "Please say hi to Babs for me," as he left.

The DI gathered up the two photographs.

"Do you think the owner is behind all this?" Rose asked.

"Rose, we think it's the obvious suspect, it's a turf war."

"So Snake?"

The DI smiled, "like many amateurs you see patterns and clues that are not really there. Police work is methodical."

"But the methods you use, who the obvious suspect is, isn't always right. After all innocent people do find themselves in prison."

"Like you claim to be, you mean?"

"I don't claim to be, I am innocent and one day I will prove it."

"Be careful Rose. My advice again, is to stay well out of it. Let me do my job."

Trixie came through to the shop as soon as she heard the inspector leave. "That was odd, aye?"

"Yes, yes, that's what I thought. It sounded as if Tony had spoken to the DI, but why pretend to you not to know? And why come in for the key then? And the picture of the owner with Troy, my ex.- he couldn't stop staring at it."

"What are ye gonnae do?"

"I need to make a call. If I have to leave, how confident are you about the biscuit dough? I can do the batters later."

"The shortbread is braw and I've just started on the chocolate cranberry. Ye want tae see?"

"I think you're good, just carry on, if you don't mind."

"Dinnae worry about me Rose, it's nae bother and I've got ma tunes."

Rose called Rob and sent a text to Marion. She had a glimmer of an idea, but she needed to be sure before she acted on it. The lock to the upstairs front door was a double, she knew there was no point in trying to open it. She looked up at the back of the building, the tiny window above the back door of the shop was shut, there was a chance she would be able to jiggle it open if the catch was as old as the window and hadn't been reinforced. The other window, which was larger, had bars on it. She climbed on to the bin, and tried to pull herself up, but she wasn't tall enough. Rob would have to lift her. She would just about fit through she thought, and he definitely wouldn't.

"I don't know Rose," he mithered at her as she told him her plan.

"Well, you want to try breaking in through the front?"

"No, but I don't get it. What are you looking for?"

"I want to know about the owner, how he knows Troy and why Tony was lying this morning. Maybe Tony knows Troy?"

"What did Marion say?"

"She's having someone go to the offices, see what they can find. She had someone go through his house the other day, but there was nothing there that connected him to me at all. Not even any old photographs. She concluded he wasn't involved after all. I agreed, I mean if he hadn't even kept a photograph … She thinks we should look upstairs."

"Alright, but not from the dumpster. Do you have cash?"

"Yes, what for?"

"I told you, you can get anything you want for money, Give me half an hour?"

It took less time than that for her phone to ping with the text, *Door's open.*

When Rose pushed on the door to the upper flat, Rob was already inside. It was dark and musky, there were boxes everywhere on the top of the landing. There were three rooms off it. Two towards the front and one at the end. The two windows at the back of the building which Rose had seen from the outside were covered in fabric which had been nailed to the wall. Rob tried one of the doors, it was unlocked. "What the …" he said as he saw the crude makeshift dry lab. Two tables with weighing scales, stainless steel measuring cups and a tablet press.

Rose pulled out her phone and started taking pictures. They went back onto the landing and tried the other doors, one of the rooms had a single bed, a counter with a microwave, a couple of plates and some food in it. The other, which housed a toilet and shower was like the landing, piled high with plastic boxes. Outside that room was a pull-down ladder leading up to the roof. Rob climbed it.

"More boxes and papers" he called down to Rose.

Rose started looking through one of the boxes on the landing. There were a group of files all numbered sequentially. She shone the torch on her phone at the outside of the other boxes. They too had numbers on them. Inside the first file was a lease, photographs of the inside of an office and two mug shots. Whoever the people in the photos were, they were young. She was about to put the file back when she realised the woman in the photograph was wearing a tiny pair of earrings with flowers on them. She squinted her good eye and focused her torch on the earrings. "Rob, this photograph, those earrings, do they look hand painted to you?"

"Rose, why are you worrying about earrings?" He leaned over to take a closer look at the photograph. "Yeah, handmade possibly. They don't look like something you'd buy in a chain store, why is it important?" Rose told Rob about the earrings the lecturer at her college had given her.

"It was the same day I met Tony. She gave them to me in front of him actually."

"So you think she's tied up in this?"

"No, no I don't. But she told me that Tony often found business premises for students who had been through her course. He didn't seem happy when she told me that, but then, when I called him he showed me the shop. Whatever is going on up here he clearly knows all about it. What are they making?"

"I don't know, it's the dry part of the process. There must be another lab for cooking somewhere else. Look at this."

Rob had gone back into the lab and opened another one of the boxes, it was full of tiny plastic bags, similar to the ones that had been taped under Rose's ottoman. Rose photo-documented the file she had opened and the box of plastic bags. Her phone pinged. It was a text from Marion, *snap.*

"What does that mean? Rob asked as Rose showed him.

"I think she must have found a picture, maybe the same one the DI showed me. I'm going to go over there and talk to her. She won't say anymore over text or on the phone."

"I'll come with you, I'm not letting you out of my sight Rose. What about Trixie, and the DI, shouldn't we tell him what we have found?"

"Yes, but you know how the police can add two and two and make five.. I want to speak to Marion first. Trixie will be fine, she's working on the biscuits. She can lock up. I'll need to come back here later too and start the batters. The shop is opening tomorrow."

"Are you sure Rose?"

"Well, that's the plan, after all, this part of the building has nothing to do with the shop. I want to make things look like business as normal, I'm sure the police will want that. I'm not going to tell Trixie what we found, by the way."

"Sure. Let's make sure we put everything back the way we found it too."

They slipped out of the front door unnoticed. Rose told Trixie she needed to go somewhere but she didn't say why. "Finish up the last dough, then go home. I'll be back later to do the batters."

"Sure Rose, what was upstairs, find onything?"

"No, just boring old paperwork."

Trixie rolled her eyes. "Weel be cannae if yous are off snooping. Ay I'll see ye the morrow."

.oOo.

Marion had sent a car to meet them at the station. The young woman who met them was smartly turned out, every inch the business professional. The car purred through Glasgow to a crescent of Georgian houses, now turned into flats. Marion was clearly doing well.

She gave Rose a picture of Troy and the shop owner as soon as they were settled inside the main living room.. "This your boy?" she asked.

"Where did you find that?"

"At Troy's office, something's written on the back."

Marion passed the picture to Rose. It was dated August 31st.

"This picture, it's dated a few days before Sally was found dead outside the shop."

"It was taken at a conference, here in Glasgow. I looked it up, the conference started on August 29th. Investing in properties. Troy was a speaker and so was this dude. There were speakers and delegates from around the world."

"I wonder if Tony was there?"

"No, well he's not on the delegate list anyway."

"How do you know that?"

"The world wide web Rose, wakey wakey. So who is Snake trying to take over from do we think? Tony, or the so-called owner of the buildings? And how does Troy figure into all this?"

"Why the *so-called* owner, Marion?"

"Just a feeling, the company is offshore so finding who the directors are is going to be a problem. This guy," she tapped the picture of the older man, "could just be being paid as a front. Tony or even Troy could be the actual owner. You don't even know that Tony is his real name."

Rose shook her head, then checked her phone for the time. "I can't believe that Tony had me fooled, I thought he was so nice, straight, just a teacher who was..-" Rose shrugged. "We should tell the DI what we found upstairs, I need to head back to the shop and get things ready for tomorrow."

"You're still opening?" Rob said.

"You betcha, that shop is my future. And whatever Tony is up to is not going to stop me."

Chapter Thirteen

January 3rd Part 2

Trixie had her earbuds in and didn't hear the bell jangle as the front door of the shop opened. The late afternoon sun had already set and she had forgotten to lock the door after Rose and Rob had left earlier. She was admiring the batches of biscuits she had made as she packed them into the bins ready for display when the shop opened the following day. It was the first time Rose had trusted her with the doughs from start to finish, and she was on a high. Zero wasted ingredients, she fist pumped, dancing on the spot then she picked up a tray of biscuits and spun round. The cloth was over her mouth before she could scream or make a move to save herself from the hypodermic needle.

.oOo.

Marion's driver drove Rose and Rob back to the station. "We can call the DI as soon as we get back to the shop, what do we say about how we got upstairs?" Rose said as they waited for the train.

"Does it matter? I mean, they'll have to get a warrant I'm guessing, I don't think they can just barge in, or can they?"

Rose pulled a face, "I think they can if they have reason to believe something's wrong. I can't get hold of Trixie, she's not picking up."

"Probably plugged into her 'tunes', as she calls them"

"Yeah probably. I hope she's alright, not fretting about the biscuits, I've been a bit of a control freak about making the dough and the batter to be honest, but she's really good. She has the knack."

It had just gone five by the time the train pulled into Haymarket and they walked the short distance from the station to the shop. The front door was locked and the place was in darkness as Rose opened up. The fragrant smell of cardamom from one of the recipes hung in the air.

"Ooh that smells good," said Rose as she went through to the back kitchen. "Well done Trixie."

Rose flicked on the light. She didn't see her at first, Trixie's crumpled little body was lying next to the freezer, she was covered in crumbled biscuits from the tray she had been holding.

"Rob, call an ambulance, she's breathing, just."

Rose couldn't stop shaking, Rob covered her with his jacket while they waited for the ambulance to arrive.

"I need a drink Rob, something."

"No Rose, that's the last thing you need, breathe in deeply, it will pass."

Rose nodded, he was right, if she drank now she would never stop. She wouldn't want to. "Why hurt her?" Rose wailed as Trixie was loaded into the ambulance and DI Chatterton arrived.

He took one look at Rose and told Rob he would have them both driven back to Rose's flat, they could speak there later. "Did she touch anything?"

"Just the light switch, nothing else," Rob said.

Rose shook her head. "I want to go to the hospital. Tell him about upstairs."

Rob explained quickly about the lab and boxes of paperwork they had found earlier. "We were going to call you as soon as we came back, but then, well then we found Trixie."

The DI shook his head. "Bloody amateurs," he sniped under his breath. "I'll be at your flat shortly, there's nothing you can do at the hospital until the doctors have done what they need to, and we have spoken to her."

Rose wanted to fight with him but she didn't have the strength. She knew he was right, she hated him for it, but she hated herself more for leaving Trixie, putting her in harm's way.

"He's right Rob," said Rose as he handed her a mug of hot tea. She was wrapped in a big woolly blanket on the sofa, still shaking, her legs tucked under her.

"No Rose, he was angry, I don't think ..."

"Yes, yes, he is right. I was arrogant, thinking I knew better, that I could solve whatever the hell is happening, and now Trixie is in hospital because of me. Four people are dead, Rob. Four!" Rose fiddled with her phone.

"What are you doing?"

"I'm texting Marion to stop digging. I don't want anything to happen to anyone else."

"Marion can take care of herself."

"I thought I could too, but this, it's a bridge too far. I'm finished."

"Rose, you're in shock, we both are. Now's not the time to give up. Trixie deserves better than that. She adores you Rose, you are her hero, we have a responsibility to her to find out who did this."

Rob was right. The hot tea felt good, she clasped it tightly, warming her hands and staring into the pale golden liquid. "So what do we know Rob? Do we know anything more that makes sense? Why would somebody try to kill Trixie."

"Because Trixie means something to you. It fits the pattern Rose. Gary's brother, Bakti and Trixie, all people that were loved, cared for."

"But we went over that before, Reynolds, Sally - they don't fit into that pattern. I mean I cared about Sally, but we weren't close, and neither of us knew Reynolds particularly."

"True. But your shop, you, are connected."

"Look the DI said they were looking at the obvious suspect, I assumed that meant Snake trying to take over running stuff here in Edinburgh. What if he is right and Snake is killing people because he still thinks I am involved somehow, trying to scare me off?"

"But he doesn't, at least Gary said he convinced him of that."

"Can you speak to him?"

"No, I don't know how to. Marion might, but I think that's the wrong route Rose, I really do. I think we need to look at Troy and Tony and whoever this owner is. How are they all connected?"

"Ok, let's make a map, a big one this time."

"How come?"

"It's like planning a flight path, you have the starting point and the destination. But sometimes things go wrong, and you need to know how to navigate your way around that."

"So, what's the starting point, captain?"

"Me," said Rose, "I am the starting point, but I also think I am the destination."

The buzzer went just as Rob had written Rose's name at the bottom of the paper where she had told him to. Rose rolled it quickly and pushed it behind the chair. It was the inspector and another detective, a sergeant.

"We need statements from both of you, about Trixie and about this morning, why you broke into the upstairs flat. Tony wants to press charges by the way, for trespass."

"What? How can he do that when ..."

"When what, Rose?"

"Well the lab, you must have found it."

"What we found was a flat full of papers about properties that Tony manages for the owner of the buildings."

Rose stared at him. "So, he knew we went up there. He moved it. But how? We were only gone a few hours."

"Look, this is what we found," Rose showed him the images on her phone.

"Where were these taken?"

"Upstairs. In the flat."

"Really, because what you are showing me could have been taken anywhere."

Rose looked at the images. He was right. She had taken everything close-up. There was no context to where anything was, no background, wall paper or windows.

"This photograph," Rose pointed to the mug shots, "Those earrings the woman is wearing, I think they were made by the same college lecturer who taught me. She knows Tony, he finds premises for students. Business premises."

"And?"

"So, he's got access to other places, that's where he would have moved the lab to."

The DI sighed, "Rose, I want to find out who attacked Trixie, attempted to kill her. None of this is helping me do that."

Rob interjected. "But we both saw it, Inspector. The lab I mean."

"What you saw and what evidence you have for what you saw are two different things. I know what I saw, or do you think I'm lying?"

"No, of course not, sorry," Rob said.

As soon as the DI and his sergeant left, Rose unrolled the paper they had begun to mark out the map on. Rose colour coded names and dates and drew connecting lines between them. She added in the lecturer from the college and the people in the photograph.

"I'll go and see her, the lecturer I mean, find out if she remembers them, what business they were starting up."

"And I'm going to go and see Troy."

"What!"

"Why not challenge him?"

"It's too dangerous, now that Tony knows we were up in the flat yesterday and we don't know if those two know each other. That's what we need to find out. How on earth did Tony find out we had been upstairs?" Then Rose looked at her phone and remembered what the painter had shown her, a hidden camera that could be viewed from anywhere.

"Of course," said Rob. "They were watching us remotely."

"Look, come with me to the college. Sarah won't have classes tomorrow, but she will probably be setting up."

"Alright, let's make that the plan then. What about Marion? Did she text you back?"

"Yes, she also sent a GIF."

Rob laughed, when Rose showed him her phone. The GIF was from an old episode of 'Bewitched'. Samantha was on a broomstick. Underneath Marion had typed Rose flies again.

"Marion's humour, on the blackest of days, it's what saw me through the last year of my sentence. Meeting Marion changed everything."

Chapter Fourteen

January 4th

Rose and Rob walked past Muffins on Morrison on their way to get the bus to the college. There was police tape over the door and a patrol car parked outside, but no sign of the DI or the sergeant. The day was gloomy, echoing what they both felt, as they looked in the windows and saw uniformed officers behind the counter.

"It's Trixie who should be standing there now," said Rose. "I hope the hospital will let us see her later. When I called, they said family only and her mum and dad are on their way. It could have been so much worse, if we hadn't come back when we did, she would be dead."

Rob put his arm over Rose's shoulder and tried to pull her close to him, for comfort. She pushed him away and they walked in silence to the college. The front doors were locked and a security guard pointed them towards a side entrance. The halls were lifeless apart from cleaners and the smell of polish. The classroom where Sarah taught was empty and dark.

"Let's go to the admin office, maybe they can locate her," Rob suggested. But as they turned to leave, Rose saw Sarah Pink walking towards them, she was trundling a suitcase and her arms were overloaded with coloured folders.

"Hello Rose, it is Rose isn't it?"

"Yes, here let me help." Rose took the bundle of folders from the lecturer's arms.

"Come in, I'm here to set up for next week. What are you doing here, is your friend going to take the programme?"

"No, nothing like that." Rose pulled out her phone, and waited until Sarah was settled before she handed it to her. "We just wondered if you might remember who these two people are, or perhaps you only know the woman. She's wearing earrings, like the ones you gave me."

Sarah put on her glasses." Let me see," she said, peering at the image on Rose's phone. "Oh yes, that's Amy, ummm Lee I think, yes Amy Lee. And her boyfriend, I can't remember his name I'm afraid, he wasn't in the class."

"Do you remember when Amy was here? She wasn't here at the same time as me."

"No, it would have been at least a year if not two before you. Let me think. I know I was fairly new, so probably six years ago. The year I started teaching here."

"And do you know what business she was starting, was she starting a business?"

"Yes, she was, it was travel. She and her boyfriend were specialising in tours to Asia. Amy said he was brought up in

Thailand, so it made sense. He did the tourism program here, while Amy did business."

"And was it Tony who found them business premises?"

"Phhh, I don't know. Tony did, as I told you, find some of the students places to rent, he seemed to have a handle on affordable accommodation and rentals. Why are you asking?" Sarah held out her hand to Rob. "I'm Sarah", "I don't think we have met before."

"Hi, Rob. I'm an old friend of Rose. Good to meet you."

"Would you know how to get in touch with Amy? I'm thinking about some international business, someone mentioned her, but they didn't know her name."

"You could try Admin, but there's confidentiality and all that, so they could only pass on your details to her. I didn't keep in touch I'm afraid. Oh wait, hang on."

Sarah opened the suitcase and took out a laptop. "This will take a few minutes, rather old I'm afraid," she said, nodding towards the laptop. "Here we go. '*The King and I Travel*', it's in the Old Town. Clever name don't you think?"

Rose smiled, "Yes, thank you Sarah. You've been really helpful."

As the two women looked at each other Rob noticed something he had never realised about Rose before.

"How's the bakery? I'm sorry I didn't make it over there, are you still on Morrison? Tony told me he had found you a place."

"Yes, yes he did. It's been good, but I might have to move, expand, that shop is a bit small now. I'll let you know." Rose was walking backwards as she spoke, her bonhomie was too fragile to remain any longer. Rob took the hint.

"Hey Rose, we'd better a run on or we will miss our next meeting."

"Yes, that's right." Turning and exiting quickly Rose blinked back the tears that were threatening to roll down her cheek from her seeing eye. She rarely made tears since she lost sight in her left eye. It wasn't a routine feature of her condition, her eye surgeon had told her, but it could happen. Seeing Sarah had reminded her of the hope she had had on that last day, despite the low grade, she had believed she was finally on the road to happiness.

"What do you want to do?" asked Rob once they were outside. "We could go to the travel shop, it's not that far."

"Yes, let's do that, do you mind if we walk, despite the weather."

"It's Edinburgh, no bad weather, just wrong clothing," he said. But the stale old joke didn't make Rose smile. "Coffee?"

"Yes," she said. "That's probably a good idea."

They were soaked through by the time they arrived at '*The King and I Travel*', boasting the promise of sunnier climes and exotic holidays from the windows. The bright red sign above the door seemed out of place in a neighbourhood aimed at tourists to Scotland competing with tartan kilts, boxes of tablet and all things Scottish.

"Are we buying a holiday or are we business owners wondering about moving nearby?"

Rob pondered Rose's question. "I think the latter, you could genuinely say you were at the same college and ran into Sarah. That way you have more leverage asking who the landlord is."

"Why don't we do it both ways. I'll go in first, then later, you can be a customer looking for a holiday."

"Sure. I'll wait in that cafe for you, then we can compare notes."

Rose was about to cross the street when Rob grabbed her arm. "Quick, let's go."

He pulled her back onto the pavement and into one of the tourist shops. "Did you see him?"

"See who? Heavens, you nearly yanked my arm out of its socket."

"Tony. Look."

Rose followed Rob's finger and saw Tony disappearing inside the travel shop.

"That was close. Do you think that's where he's moved the lab to?"

Rose shrugged. "Well, if those files are anything to go by he has access to any number of properties. But it has to be more than a coincidence he came here this morning, just after we spoke to Sarah, and just after he's cleared out the flat at Morrison. Do you think Sarah called the shop?"

Rose wrinkled her nose. "I don't think so, Rob. But perhaps I'm not such a good judge of character these days. Look, he's leaving. He didn't have that case with him before did he?"

"No, he most certainly didn't," said Rob as they watched Tony pull a large black suitcase through the door behind him.

"Change of plan, one of us needs to follow him. It looks like he's going away, if he is we need to know where to."

"I'll do that, you try and find out more about the travel business. Sorry Rose, do you have any money?"

Rose handed him a credit card, it was the one she kept at her flat for emergencies. It was all she had until the new cards to replace the ones that were stolen came through. "Use this, 7891. Got it?"

Rob ducked out of the shop and disappeared after Tony. Rose sent him a text with the code she had just given him, she doubted he would remember the numbers, it had all happened so fast.

She waited until they were both out of sight then crossed the street and made a point of looking at the holidays on offer in the windows, trying to see who was inside. From the description Sarah had given them, a diminutive dark-haired woman in her late twenties, the woman organising brochures just behind the front desk was Amy.

Rob's journey on foot was short and he was glad of the credit card when he saw Tony hailing a taxi. Rob scanned the traffic, looking for another free taxi, ironically looking forward to the driver's response as he gave the instruction, "follow that cab."

Rose pushed open the door, the promise of paradise and luxury screamed at her from the huge posters covering each of the three inner walls of the shop. Amy was alone in the front of the shop but Rose could hear a man talking on the phone from the back room, accessed by a dark cavity in the middle of the back wall.

"How can I help?" Amy's cheerful voice reflected the mood of the smiling travellers on the brochures she was holding.

Rose took a breath and glanced behind her as she decided how to play the scene either as a potential traveller or former student? She decided on the latter, "Great location you have."

"Thanks, are you looking for a holiday, where are you thinking about going?"

Rose pulled a business card from her bag, "No, I'm here about something else. My name is Rose, I'm also a business owner, Sarah Pink from the college mentioned you to me. We did the same course. I make muffins, biscuits, I am just wondering about moving up here, into the Old Town. I wondered how you found it, the location I mean?"

"Sarah? I haven't seen her since I left," Amy put her head to one side. Her demeanour changed, her body stiffened when Rose had mentioned Sarah. "Why did she mention me?"

"Umm, just when I told her I was thinking about moving into this area."

"Can I help?" A tall athletic man came through from the back. He was well dressed but casual, as if he were about to take off on one of the holidays.

"This is Rose," said Amy handing the man the business card. "Thinking about moving her business near here."

He looked at the card and shrugged, "Mostly tourists around here."

"But your business, surely you attract local customers?"

"We mostly look after foreign nationals and business customers who want a specialised service. I don't think we can help you." He walked closer to Rose, his presence was unsettling, he clearly wanted her to leave.

"Goodbye Rose, I'm sure you'll find somewhere, Edinburgh has so many lovely parts to it." Amy said brightly and returned her attention to the brochures.

Rose looked down, what was it she had said that had created such a strange response? As soon as she exited the door, the man changed the *Welcome, come in* sign to *Sorry, we are closed*. Rose sent a text to Rob.

Travel agency, very odd. Where are you?

But he didn't text back. Rose began walking back to her flat, she didn't have the strength to pass her shop and took a longer route, looking up at the various buildings and businesses, wondering which ones might be owned by the man in the picture DI Chatterton had shown her, and what Tony's real role in all of this was. He was fit, but he was an unlikely killer. And what about Babs, was that sweet gentle exterior a front too?

Rose was almost home when the DI called her. "Rose, can you come down to the station?"

"Sure, is it urgent, should I come now?"

"Please Rose, shall I send a car?"

"No, I'm out walking, it's fine."

She was almost at the police station when Rob sent a text. "He's on his way to Singapore, he's checking in from Edinburgh Airport now."

Rose quickly texted back. "On my way to see the DI, I'll tell him. Text the flight number."

The DI was clearly not pleased with her. He came straight to the point as the uniformed officer led her into the interview room where he was already waiting. "What were you doing at that travel agency this morning?"

"How did you know?"

"I'm asking the questions, Rose. What are you playing at?"

"I'm trying to find out what happened to Trixie and all the other people who have been killed since September. You seem to be looking in the wrong direction!"

"And your meddling has just blown months of work. Thank you. Why did you go there Rose, or do I have to charge you with obstruction?"

"No, but you should know this." She pulled out her phone displaying Rob's last texts and handed it to the DI.

"Wait here." He took the phone and left the room. Rose looked around, the uniformed officer sat silently and still behind her. When the DI came back he seemed even more exasperated. "So, Rob followed Tony? Is that right?"

Rose nodded, "We went to see if we could find out who owned the building, if the lab could have been moved there?"

"What led you there, or should I say who?"

"My old teacher at the college, Sarah Pink, knew that Tony had helped one of the students find a place to rent for her travel shop. But when I got there, it was very weird. Amy, the girl Sarah had told me about was fine, but whoever was there with her, maybe it was her boyfriend, well my being there upset him."

"Yes, you did. That's not all you've upset. So it was because of this teacher that you went there? No other reason?"

"No, just to see if we could find out who the owner is, like I told you, you didn't believe us about the lab, I needed proof."

"Rose, when we first met, do you remember me telling you that we don't always discuss police business with anyone outside?"

"Yes," Rose stared at him, then nodded. "I get it. Just because you didn't tell me, doesn't mean you didn't already know."

"To be fair, your photographs were helpful. We had no way of requesting access before yesterday. But what you did was set off a chain of events that has interrupted months of an undercover investigation."

"Is that why they attacked Trixie?" Rose gasped, she couldn't bear it and struggled to breath. Her heart was beating faster and faster.

But the DI shook his head, "No, hurting her makes no sense at all. She clearly didn't hear anyone moving about upstairs in the afternoon after you left."

"None of the deaths make sense either, well except perhaps for Dr Reynolds."

"Why him?"

"Because he started working for Snake?"

"How do you know that?"

"I don't for sure. But why Sally, Bakti, Gary's brother?"

The DI slid some of the papers in front of him over to Rose."

"Do you recognise any of this?"

Rose sifted through the pile of papers, each containing the image of a cheque with her signature on the bottom. But it wasn't her signature. The little circle dot she used as she turned the pen back across her name wasn't quite right. And the bank account, the cheques were drawn from a bank she had never heard of. The cheques were for £500, dated since she had started renting both premises. The last one was drawn on December 1st. The cheques were all made out to a Mr Fraser Hamilton. "Is that the man who owns the property? I don't understand, I can show you my bank statements."

"I will need to see them. But can you confirm whether this is your signature?"

"It definitely isn't."

"Alright Rose, thanks. That's all I needed to verify and please, stay out of things."

"But, what about Trixie?"

"All in good time Rose. We will get there, Methodology remember, it's a process."

Rose nodded, biting her lip. The DI's answer was not good enough, but she wasn't going to tell him that. As she left the police station she sent Marion a text. *Fraser Hamilton?* Then she sent another text to Rob. *Going back to see Sarah Pink. Meet you at the flat, can you pick up food with my CC. Rx*

.oOo.

"Hello again Rose." Sarah looked pleased to see her, she was half-way up a ladder, pinning the interactive tools she used when she was teaching. "You've just caught me, I'm about finished for the day."

"Fancy a coffee?"

"Sure, I've got a bit of time before I need to run home and walk the wee beastie."

Rose smiled. She had seen pictures of Sarah's westie on her screen saver when the PowerPoint reverted to Sarah's home screen. "What's its name?"

"Hamish, not very original, but it suits him."

They walked to the cafe in silence. Rose was wondering how she was going to ask Sarah whether she had called Amy that morning and what she really knew about Tony. Sarah was humming. The cafe was getting ready to close, but the woman behind the counter pointed to the shelf by the window with high stools. "Ye can sit doon there, if ye are just wanting drinks. Nae food the noo, I'm afraid."

The women settled themselves, Rose put her bag on her lap and started fiddling with the zipper. There was an awkward silence between them until Sarah spoke up.

"So, how come I don't see you for years then twice in one day?" Sarah said, dunking the finger of shortbread that accompanied the latte.

Rose decided to launch straight into why she was there. "How well do you know Tony? What do you know about him?"

Sarah pulled a face. "What's this about Rose? I didn't buy the story about your visit this morning, and why you brought that fellow Rob, with you."

"Did you call Amy and let her know I was coming over?"

Sarah didn't answer.

"Sarah, please it's important."

"Look Rose, I don't know what it is you're doing, but Amy is a nice girl and she's done well. I thought this," she gestured to the coffee, "was because you wanted to see me. I honestly haven't stopped thinking about you since the last time we met, do you remember?"

Rose nodded. "Yes. Sarah, you knew where I was, you could have come to see me, if you really wanted to."

"But I couldn't, I was your teacher. I had to wait for you, but you never came."

"Well, not after I had completed the course you weren't. But probably it was best. As you say you were my teacher and I'm … I'm complicated, to be friends with I mean."

Sarah stared at Rose, "But not with Rob, the man who was with you this morning." Her face was sharp as she almost spat the words. Her eyes went backwards and forwards.

Rose sipped her tea, uncomfortable by the way Sarah was behaving. "Rob and I go way back."

Sarah's response was curt, like a disappointed parent or lover feeling they had been lied to, "I see."

Rose pulled her bag over her head, getting ready to leave. The meeting was turning weird, she didn't like the vibe she was feeling. Sarah's possessiveness reminded her of Troy. "You clearly don't want to help, so I'll go. But Sarah, just so you know, Tony isn't what he seems, perhaps you already know that." Rose slipped off the stool and left the cafe without giving Sarah the chance to reply.

She had had several texts from Rob while she was with Sarah, mostly about food, then.

That girl, the one from the travel agency, she's here, outside the flat. Shall I let her in?

Yes, on my way, she texted back. Rose walked as fast as she could back to the flat.

Rob had settled Amy in the living room and was pouring her a tea when Rose arrived.

"Amy, this is a surprise."

Amy looked at Rob and then back at Rose.

"Sorry about this morning."

"What exactly are you sorry about, Amy?" said Rose as she sat next to her on the sofa. "And how did you know where I lived?"

"From some paperwork. It was in some files Alan, he is my boyfriend, kept locked in his desk. He had pulled them out to show Tony, they were talking about you when he came to get the bag he kept in the office. He uses it whenever he travels to Singapore."

"Why does he keep the bag there? What did he say about me?"

"He was shouting, he said the plans needed to change, that Alan had messed up."

"What plans, what had Alan messed up?"

"I don't know. Afterwards, after you left, Alan got really nasty. I'd never seen him like that before, he started accusing me of betraying him and everything he was working for. Your presence seemed to really unsettle him. I tried to calm him down, tell him I hadn't met you before or seen Sarah since college, but he left, and now I don't know where he is, he took his phone, his wallet and a lot of cash out of our business account. Well, all of it."

"So why come here, why not go to the police?"

"Because I found this." Amy opened her bag and took out an envelope. Inside the envelope was a passport with Amy's photograph and the name Leanne Boyd."

"What the heck, first cheques with my supposed signature and now a false passport."

Rose handed the passport to Rob.

"Looks pretty authentic."

"Where was it?"

"It was at our flat, where we keep all the important documents, Alan's passport is missing. I guess he took it. I went there thinking that's where he had gone after he left the shop."

"What cheques?" asked Rob.

"The police have them, they are all dated on the first of the month for £500 made out to someone called Fraser Hamilton."

"He's the building owner, our building I mean," Amy said.

"Have you met him?"

"Yes, but not until last year, it was at a property thing, Tony asked us to go for him, he couldn't make it."

"When was this?"

"Last August."

"What were you supposed to do?"

"Put in offers on certain properties, there was a list."

"Was it him?" Rose pulled the photograph Marion had given her from a file lying on the table.

"Yes, that's him, that's Fraser Hamilton" Amy pointed at the picture of Troy.

Rose frowned, looked across at Rob, and then pointed at the older man Troy was shaking hands with. "Do you know who he is?"

"He was one of the speakers, but I don't remember his name."

"How many identities does Troy have?" Rob said.

"Who is Troy?" Amy asked.

"That's a good question, Amy. That's who I knew this man as. But you haven't really answered my question from before, why did you come here?"

Amy looked down, Rose knew that look. The hunch, the feeling of shame.

"Is it your boyfriend? Something else, not just from today?"

Amy nodded, "I knew the business couldn't be doing as well as he kept saying. We seemed to have more money than made sense, I was the one who was supposed to be running that side of things. But he took over, almost straight away after we finished college, and I ended up selling the holidays. He and Tony would travel together sometimes, sometimes Babs and I went, that was before she got sick, but Tony and Alan always had meetings outwith the hotels or apartments where we stayed. When I tried to remind him we were partners he always made it seem like I was being churlish, ungrateful that he was taking care of things while I could just enjoy the holiday. And then, since last August, after we came back from the conference, things really changed. He became aggressive, stayed out late, or didn't tell me where he was going. I thought it was an affair, but he denied that."

Rose's phone pinged, it was Marion. The reply to her text said *Troy!* The text followed with an image of Fraser Hamilton/aka Troy from a newspaper clipping dated three years earlier.

Rose handed her phone to Rob and then showed Amy.

"How do you know him?" Amy asked.

"We were engaged, and a lot else, he set me up, I went to prison for three years because of him."

Amy stared at Rose, "I am really afraid what Alan has been doing is going to land him there too. I feel stupid, I trusted him. I couldn't take prison."

"You'd be surprised what you can survive Amy when you have to." said Rose.

Amy stared at her. "You? You were in prison?"

"It's how I ended up on the course and was able to set up my business. I applied to a grant for ex-offenders. Does that bother you?"

"Yes, no, I don't know...-"

"It's ok Amy, do you want to leave?"

"No, I'm sorry, it was just a shock."

"I understand. This is what I think we need to do, but we need to do it fast. Whatever Tony meant about plans changing, this passport, we need to get one step ahead, stop whatever it is they are up to, and then tell the police."

"Shouldn't we tell the police first?" said Rob.

"No. The DI made it clear that I am persona non grata and that our so-called meddling has interrupted their investigation, but what if, what if they have been looking in all the wrong places?"

"OK, what do you want to do, Rose?" Rob said.

.oOo.

It was gone midnight by the time Rose had finished outlining her plan to him.. Amy had fallen asleep on the sofa and Rose didn't have the heart to wake her.

"I think we can trust her, Rob." Rose said as they left the girl asleep and headed out into the street.

Chapter Fifteen

Troy's Glasgow offices were on the third floor, there had been no way into the building from the ground floor because of the security guard. Rose crawled in through a basement window Troy's business used for storage. She was surprised to find the catch was still broken after all these years, but then Troy never was good at paying attention to things he felt were beneath him. There was a window at the top of the stairwell leading to a fire escape at the back, from which she managed to lever herself onto the ledge outside the windows of Troy's suite. She had always had a good head for heights, but since her eye problems she wasn't as brave as her former glory days when leaping out of a plane hadn't been an issue. "Don't look down" she muttered to herself .

She knew Troy's window would be secure, he rarely let in fresh air, complaining of cold and draughts. She just hoped the admin staff weren't so cautious. Rob was waiting down below. He had tried to dissuade her from coming herself, to let Marion send someone instead but Rose was adamant, it had to be her on the basis she would know what she was looking for when she saw it. Rose was out of luck with the windows, they were all locked tight. Rose made her way back down the ledge to the fire escape and was about to repeat the exercise on the floor below when she felt her phone vibrate with a text.

The guard, he's leaving.

Rose checked the time, cover was supposed to be twenty-four hours, night and day, if the guard had slipped out it was likely that he would have switched the cameras off, so he wasn't caught skiving. She made her way back down to the basement, through to the reception and up the main staircase inside the building and used her credit card to slip the lock to Troy's suite. Even in the dark Rose could tell nothing much had changed. Troy was a creature of habit and obsessive about order, Rose felt under his desk.

She smiled to herself, "Thank you Troy, still a creature of habit!" she muttered as she took the key which was taped under it and unlocked the top drawer of his desk. There she found the rest of the keys in a blue leather pouch.

Rose set to work, she was methodical, perhaps it was RAF training, she knew it was essential nothing was disturbed or not put back the way she found it. She had about two hours before the cleaning staff arrived. She texted Rob.

I'm in.

Her initial optimism faded as she searched file after file, finding nothing that linked Troy to Tony. She opened the last file and was about to put it back when she saw the small envelope, yellowed with age tucked into the back. The rest of the contents of the file was all about Troy, his certificates and qualifications as a financial advisor. Rose opened the envelope carefully, there were three different photographs of Troy aged about four or five. He was alone, sitting by a sandcastle on a beach in the first one, but in the other two pictures a different lone adult was with him, their arms wrapped around him wearing a big towel. Babs was in one picture and Tony was in the other. Rose stared at the images, then grabbed her phone and photographed them. Her phone vibrated.

Guard's back.

Damn it, she would have to go out through the ledge but at least the risk had been worth it, she wasn't sure quite how yet, but she felt closer to some sort of solution as she clambered through the admin office window and closed it. Distracting herself from the height as she crawled back along the ledge to the fire escape Rose wished she had Poirot's little grey cells. To her memory he had never had to risk life and limb on the narrow ledge of a building to solve who killed who.

"Look what I found," Rose showed Rob the photographs she had taken of the three pictures.

"I don't believe it, so Troy is Patrick?"

"Well, Troy always claimed he didn't know his parents and Tony and Babs have only ever mentioned Patrick, but I never saw a picture of him come to think of it. They have no visible memories of their child on display anywhere in the flat. Isn't that odd?"

"Maybe it was too painful."

"For Babs maybe, but I have a feeling Tony has known that Patrick and Troy were the same person, for a lot longer than since last August."

"What makes you think that? Look, let's not stand here, someone might see us, the city is waking up."

It was still dark but Rob was right, the 5am workforce, buses and cars were evident. "We can talk on the train back to Haymarket."

"And hopefully, after that we can go and see Trixie, she might know who attacked her. I just hope the police are keeping her safe."

"I hope you were right about being able to trust Amy," he said, "my gut is telling me we shouldn't have left her." But by the time they arrived back at Rose's flat his gut had proved wrong. Amy was still at the flat, she was adding some information of her own to the map Rose and Rob had started, about her boyfriend Alan.

Rose phoned the hospital. "Nothing yet, she's still unconscious, although it's an induced coma, they are hoping she will be awake later today or tomorrow."

"How did you find that out, I thought they would only speak to family?"

Rose shrugged, "Well a concerned sister calling from abroad ..."

"The DI will kill you if he finds out," said Rob.

"Well maybe if he did his job better."

"That's a bit harsh Rose, but I agree, it does seem to be taking them time to make sense of everything."

Rose looked at the notes about Alan that Amy had added. Born in Thailand to British expats, he had gone to boarding school in England, then went travelling, before going to college. He had met Amy on holiday in a resort. It was one of the resorts they returned to after setting up the travel business; it was where they met Tony and Babs. Tony had suggested the college programme and the travel business to Alan. He hadn't expected Amy to get involved.

"How did you and Tony and Babs get talking, after all, there's quite an age difference?"

Amy nodded, "It was Tony and Alan who met first in the bar, then we were invited to dinner."

"Did they ever mention a son, Patrick?"

"No, well I think Babs may have when I asked her if she had any children, but Tony - well, come to think of it, Tony seemed to change the subject."

"And how did the conversation about college and travel start? Was that from Tony?"

"Yes, when he learned that Alan was well connected in Thailand through his parents, he told us that he knew lots of business people who would be interested in specialist travel around Asia; Alan would be an asset because he was fluent in several languages, but was also British. But last night, you mentioned the name Troy, and I didn't think of it until this morning, but I think it was at dinner a few months ago when that name came up and Tony got really mad with Babs. It was very uncomfortable. Alan and I left the table until they had sorted things out. Sorry, I wish I knew more, but we left the room."

"Where was this?"

"It was in Singapore. That's where we also saw this man," she pointed to the picture of the older man in the picture with Troy. "But we didn't meet with him, he met with Tony alone. We only saw him once and I was too upset last night to make the connection, that he was the same man who spoke at the conference in Glasgow."

"Have you ever heard of someone called Snake?" Rose asked.

"Well, Alan ..."

"Alan what?" asked Rob.

"Alan mentioned him. Alan and Tony had another row. It was at the shop and they asked me to leave, when I came back I heard Alan talking to someone on the phone. He said the word Snake, I thought he was talking about someone being a snake, he was using Thai to whoever he was speaking to. He wasn't happy when he realised I had overheard the conversation. It was the first time I felt unsafe with him actually. But then he turned on the charm and of course, I thought it was my fault, for being nosey."

"Where is this getting us?" asked Rob. "It feels like we are creating a different map somehow."

"No, it's all connected," said Rose. Her face was set as she pulled the map towards her and examined the lists and the notes Amy had made. "Here's what we have," she said, handing paper and a pen to Rob.

"Tony, Troy/Patrick, Sarah, Alan and this man, she pointed to the photograph let's call him T, for Tanned, all know each other and are connected in business through property and who knows what else, but definitely drugs. Rob, can you make a new list with those names please? And then, a second list with Snake, Gary, Alan, Reynolds and Troy on it."

"Wait, what's the connection between Troy and Snake?"

"I don't know, so put a question mark, it's just a feeling. Rob, could Snake have been supplying Troy back when I was with him, when you stopped? He was from Glasgow after all?"

"I don't know Rose, I didn't know him then, he approached me when he came to Edinburgh."

"But how did he know you? You were hardly a dealer really. Why bother with someone as small as you?"

"Do you think Troy told him about me?"

"The one constant throughout this for me is that it feels familiar. That what's happening around me, around you is a set up. I just can't ignore it anymore, especially now that we know Troy and Tony know each other, or worse, that Troy is probably Patrick, Tony's son."

"And Sarah?" asked Amy. "You think she is somehow involved.?"

"I hope not, but why did she feel the need to tell you, or Alan that I was coming over and why did she make things for only some of the students? It didn't occur to me that perhaps that was a sign for Tony, who he should approach?"

"But I already knew him, I told you we knew him from before college."

"True, I'd still like to know who else she gave them to though. Whether they were involved with Tony somehow. Did she pick students opening businesses that would somehow serve him, like with all the cheques in my name. What the heck is that all about?"

"Financial stuff, that's more Troy, surely," said Rob.

"Maybe. Amy, could you go to the college, don't talk to Sarah, but see if you can find out the students that graduated since Sarah worked there, say you're planning a reunion or something. Now that the police have finished in the shop I am going to go and prepare to open again tomorrow."

"What!" Rob looked shocked as the word flew out of his mouth.

"It's the only way to flush out whoever is behind this, to make them think I'm still a threat to be dealt with or whatever. I'll tell the DI, don't worry, I am sure it's the right thing to do. For Trixie."

"Well in that case maybe I should talk to Troy, beard the lion so to speak."

"No, but there is something I would like you to do, Rob. You'll think it's mad but I want to know why my father has always insisted my mother wasn't killed because she fell down the stairs. What is it that has bugged him all these years? Would you go and see him for me, in Bristol?"

"Of course, Rose, if you think he will speak to me."

"Make up whatever you have to, to make him. Tell him you and I have fallen out if you want."

"What's this about Rose?" asked Amy.

"I don't know, it could be nothing, but in the back of my mind I always questioned what it was that made him convinced I had something to do with her death, when the coroner, the police, all said it was a fatal accident and I was so many miles away. A tragedy, the way we were supposed to think about Sally, remember Rob, you used those exact words."

Rob nodded and checked his watch. "It's just after 10, if I leave now, I could catch the 10.52 cross country train and be there late this afternoon. I'd have to travel back tomorrow though."

"Thank you. You'll need my credit card. Just don't travel first class please."

Rob smiled, "You know me, I'm a cheap date, I'll text you."

"I'll get off as well Rose, will you be at the shop for the rest of the day?" Amy said.

"Yes, well at least until it's possible to go to the hospital, if it is. Let me know what you find out and here," Rose handed Amy one of the spare keys to the flat. "You can stay here, I'm not sure it's a good idea for you to go back to the flat you share with Alan, I mean, if you want."

"Thanks Rose, but I think he's left Edinburgh, and he has no idea what has happened since yesterday, when you came to the shop."

"All the same Amy, we don't know who attacked Trixie, and what or who else Alan was involved with."

"Alright, I'll need some clothes though. What should I say if Sarah sees me at the college?"

"You know, second thoughts, why don't you phone the admin department instead, then you can use my computer to do a search for any of the names of companies."

"You really think she has something to do with this? She seemed so nice."

"Yes, so did Tony."

"True, alright, let me see how I get on."

Rose called the DI and left a message to confirm she had received his message about opening up the shop and was heading there now. She also let him know she had connected her ex to Tony, that she thought they were father and son. She was curious about DI Chatterton, he seemed very experienced to still be a DI and surely this was a major investigation? Who was he answerable to, she wondered.

When Rose arrived at the shop she busied herself cleaning the detritus left from the police. When she opened the kitchen her eyes immediately fell on the scattered biscuits all over the floor and the trays Trixie had set out, ready for boxing. Everything would have to be thrown away now. Rose felt as if she was betraying Trixie as she binned all her hard work. "You did good Trixie," she said softly as she picked up one of the decorated macadamia nut biscuits and examined it for colour and texture.

It was mid-afternoon by the time Rose finished cleaning and started making batters. She was exhausted, emotionally and physically drained and was about to make a brew when the DI arrived.

"I heard your message, how did you find out the two men are related. Bit more than a coincidence isn't it?"

Rose nodded, "Tea? I am about to make one for myself."

"Thanks. I will."

Rose showed the DI the photograph on her phone as they settled at the small table by the shop window.

"How did you get this?"

"Mmmm, can't remember," Rose said, pursing her lips and flushing.

"Come on Rose!"

"You won't like it and you won't be able to use it as evidence if I tell you."

"I doubt I can use it anyway, evidence for what?"

"That Troy is behind all this, Trixie, Sally, Gary's brother."

The DI sighed. "Rose, you have to stop putting the working parts of an investigation, my investigation I might add, in the wrong order. There is no reason to think that Troy has played any part in what's been happening in Edinburgh. And you've not answered my question. Where did you get the picture?"

"Troy's office."

"You broke in?"

Rose blinked and the inspector shook his head at her. "I told you, you wouldn't like my answer."

Rose stuck out her chin as the inspector sighed into the steaming cup of tea Rose had poured for him. She was irritated that he was right, she hadn't provided any evidence about Troy and what her gut was telling her. But then, the police hadn't listened to her protests of innocence about Troy setting her up before, nor had they listened to her father, about her mother and his feeling that the fall was just not right.

The DI stood up, "I'm sorry about Trixie, Rose and that you seem to think I am not doing my job. I can assure you I am."

"Can I ask you something?"

"You can ask, I might not answer."

"Why Scotland? Why are you here, not working down in England? Essex - is that right?"

"You have a good ear, Essex and Suffolk borders actually. Why do you want to know?"

"Because, well this is going to sound rude, you seem a bit old, perhaps experienced is better, to still be a DI and yet there's been no one higher working on this."

"Police business," he said and left. There was no clue from his expression that Rose had touched a nerve about his rank.

Rose sent Rob a text then set about making the batters and a couple of biscuit doughs. It would be slim fare on offer when she opened, but at least by baking she could take a brief break from perseverating about murder and who was behind all of them.

Later, when Rose arrived home and she and Amy were discussing what Amy had found out, Rob pinged back with a photograph and a question.

Do you recognise this?

The image was of a tiny seahorse charm with a sapphire eye. Her parents had given it to Rose when she was eighteen. They had been on holiday in Majorca and brought it back for her.

Yes, I lost it years ago. Rose replied, expanding the image to examine it more closely. If it wasn't the one she had lost it was identical.

It was in your mother's pocket the day she died. The police didn't think it was important, but that's why your father has been convinced you were there that day, at the house. And there was a woman, he had never seen her before, but she said she had seen a girl leaving the house earlier, she described you. Unfortunately, he didn't get her name and the police couldn't find anyone that looked like her living near by. He told me that no one believed much that he said, and he didn't really believe the police had followed up."

"What! Are you still with him?

No, I'm on my way back, I'll stay near the station and get the 6am. Rose, you should call him. He is not doing well.

OK. Thanks Rob, see you tomorrow.

Chapter Sixteen

January 6th

Rose tossed and turned all night, thinking about her mother and the picture Rob had sent her. She racked her brains trying to remember when she had last worn the seahorse charm, it seemed to vanish after she wore it to a party with Troy, they had both got very drunk and had a row. How on earth could it have ended up in her mother's pocket, why was this the first time she had heard about it and who was the woman who had spoken to her father?

Frustrated by her commitment to open the shop, Rose was torn whether to send the picture of the charm to DI Chatterton or not, prompt him to see what he could find about the witness who had supposedly seen her. The police had clearly ignored the significance of the charm before, why would they take notice now after all these years? Rob's train was due in just after one o'clock. It had been too late to call her father last night, after she and Rob had texted and it now seemed too early to call him before she left for the shop.

Rose slipped out of the flat leaving Amy asleep, she was still loath to sleep on the bed and they had both shared the sofa in the living room. When she woke Amy was going to spend the morning contacting the businesses she had found from her discussion with the admin department at the college.

It would be hard juggling serving and baking without Trixie with so much on her mind. She desperately wanted to see Trixie, but the hospital and the police were still restricting visits to family only while she was unconscious. Rose arrived at the shop to find a formal notice stuck to the windows and a chain and padlock barring her way to the front door. The notice stated that the premises and assets of the building had been seized by order of the court. Rose wasn't sure whether to laugh or cry, the irony of wishing she hadn't prepared for opening and now this. How much more could she take she thought as she trudged back to the flat.

"What's happened?" asked Amy as Rose let herself back in.

"The shop, I'm barred from entry, or getting any of my stuff. I have no idea why, the names on the order were solicitors, I'm going to call them and the DI."

"But I thought Tony owned the building?"

"Well not according to him or the police, but yes, I think he does really."

The telephone number for the solicitors greeted Rose with a recorded message. "The offices were not open for calls until 9.30am".

"Useless," Rose yelled. She felt like throwing her phone across the room. She was becoming agitated and she recognised the tell tales signs that would lead to her downfall if she let them. She dialled her sponsor.

Amy tried hard not to listen as Rose unburdened herself to the woman at the other end of the phone. She could tell it was touch and go, that Rose was on the point of giving up. Amy knew addiction second hand, she had seen it ruin the lives of friends and she had been worried about Alan, despite his protestations that he could take it or leave it. She boiled the kettle and hunted around the kitchen to create a breakfast. Amy put the plates of eggs, toast and avocado on the table and whipped the steaming mugs of hot chocolate, hoping the aroma would distract Rose and they could talk, at least until Rob came back.

Rose could feel her confidence ebbing away as she clung onto the mug of chocolate. The bittersweet taste of the cocoa reminded her of one of the first baking lessons she had attended at the prison, pouring melted chocolate onto the base of the Florentine biscuits for the visitors centre Christmas party six years ago. She hadn't known then that it would be baking that would help her heal herself and help her help others too.

"Thank you for this Amy," she said softly. "It was an inspired choice."

Amy smiled, "My mother used to say that, when I cooked for her, I mean. She had depression, there were certain foods that helped, chocolate was one. Do you want to talk more about it, about how you are feeling?"

Rose shook her head "No, I want to try and refocus, get this puzzle done once and for all and then I want my shop back. Well maybe not that shop, I think too much has happened there."

"We could always try Feng Shui to get rid of the bad memories, even here, we could try it in the bedroom."

Rose put her head on one side and looked at the young woman opposite her. She was tiny compared to Rose, clearly smart, and stunning, the way dual heritage children always seemed to be. Asian and Caucasian, Rose was curious about from where, but it was too awkward to ask.

"And what about you Amy, will you use Feng Shui at your flat, or at the business you own with Alan?"

"I don't know. I've tried to text Alan but there's been no reply. I should go to the shop though, there are bookings and I need to sort out the money he has taken, some of that was held in trust."

"I'm sorry Amy, if me blundering in there caused that."

"Well no, clearly whatever Alan has going on with Tony did that."

"Let's get to work, no more pity party, just make me hot chocolate if I look grim. Deal?"

"Deal!"

Rose and Amy clinked mugs, cleared off the table and then set to work tracking, tracing and trying to put the pieces of what they knew together. Rose called the DI to explain what had happened to her shop and the charm Rob had found out about when he saw her father.

"It appears that Edinburgh Investments and Lettings PLC have declared themselves bankrupt." Rose said as soon as she had finished her call with the DI. "There are fifteen locations all closed up this morning, following court orders made yesterday. Amy, do any of these locations match the businesses you were tracking?"

Amy checked the notes Rose gave her against the names of the businesses she had been trying to contact. "All of them. What does it mean?"

"It means that whoever is behind Edinburgh Investments, let's speculate it is Tony, is moving his business elsewhere, that Edinburgh is too hot now. Somehow, he was using the new businesses that the students were setting up as a cover, I don't know exactly what for, but I am guessing money laundering because of the cheques the DI showed me, and drugs."

"Our business, The King and I, that building is on this list too." Amy said. "So no point me going there. I think I am in big trouble."

"We need to know who the directors of Edinburgh Investments are, Marion told me it was an offshore company. Amy, how did you set up the travel company? I mean did you have money, did someone invest?"

"I had the inheritance from my parents and Alan had a business loan."

"Tony didn't give you money?"

"Well not exactly but you mentioned cheques. He did put cheques through the business."

"How do you mean?"

"Well, he would ask Alan to cash a cheque, but the accounts were not in his name, the cheque was signed by someone else to him."

"Were they large amounts?"

"No, usually about £500 every month."

"£500?"

"Yes, why?"

"That's the same amount that the cheques the DI have in my name are for. So if we assume that he was somehow taking a tax free five hundred from the fifteen businesses that are now closed, plus yours and mine that's seventeen times £500 a month, just over 100K a year cash."

"But the money didn't really exist, did it?"

"It must have, if the cheques didn't bounce. Perhaps that's how he paid the other man in the photograph? Or he was laundering it somehow from somewhere else, possibly drugs. I don't exactly know how all that works."

"Me either, but the money obviously came from somewhere or someone."

"Mmm it is a significant amount of cash to have available every year. But how do the cheques tie in with the murders?"

"I think I can answer that," said Rob. They hadn't heard him let himself back into the flat. He was soaking wet and dripping everywhere, his face was alive with excitement. "While I was waiting for the train I spent the time trying to contact Gary. I found him eventually, he's really scared, it seems his brother wasn't quite the innocent victim we all thought. His business had always seemed extremely profitable according to Gary, yet there was no money when he died, even for a funeral. His parents had to pay for it, but guess who his investor or silent business partner turned out to be?"

Rose and Amy looked at him expectantly as he paused. "Can't you guess?"

"Come on Rob, what do you know?"

"Troy, or rather Fraser Hamilton, was Gary's brother's business partner. Gary had no idea."

"So Gary's brother wasn't killed to warn Gary, it was because he was involved somehow. But why put him in my flat? We need to start again, our reasoning for why the murders were happening, why I was kidnapped, doesn't make sense at all now."

"I agree," said Rob. "But there's something else. I'm sorry Rose." Rob took a breath, his voice was shaky as he spoke. "Bakti saw two men put Sally outside your shop, he confided in Gary and Gary told his brother, Gary assumed it was Snake. Bakti was afraid to go to the police. I think he tried to tell me that night, after we saw you. But I wasn't in the mood for serious, and we got high. I only just put the pieces together after I spoke to Gary. Bakti didn't know who either of the men were, he was just looking out of the building waiting for me,"

Rose cleared off the table and spread out the last map they had been working on trying to see a different pattern, approaching each formula like she would a new recipe; adding a dash of this or a touch or that made the world of difference to something tasty and delicious versus unappetising stodge. Amy tried calling some of the business numbers she had for the former students, but none of them were working. Rob began making a timeline of events on the wall, where Rose had pinned her original lists.

"Can you add my mother's death onto that Rob. She died eight years ago, on the 25th May."

Rob nodded. He had thought the trip to Bristol had been a wild goose chase, and he still couldn't see why Rose thought there was a connection to what had happened then. "I still don't see how your mum's death could be tied up with all this Rose."

The DI had repeatedly stated methodology was the only way to solve a crime. Rose deliberated on every detail, changing the order of names, making different connections between Tony, Sarah, Troy, Snake and Doctor Reynolds. Finally, she had a pattern that made sense, along with Rob's timeline.

"Amy, can you try and get in touch with Alan again, if he answers see if you can find out where he is and see if he knows about the building being closed. Tell him you went there and found the notice."

"Ok, but all his social media has been quiet since he left and he hasn't answered any of my texts so far."

"Well just text him about the building, see if he responds. Then can you phone the college again, ask to speak to Sarah, but hang up if they put you through."

Rose had two pieces of paper in her hand, she waited for Amy to finish the text and phone calls before she placed them on the map.

"No reply from Alan and according to the college admin Sarah hasn't turned up to teach her class today."

Rose dialled the hospital. Trixie was still unconscious. "OK so Trixie can't confirm what I think I know about who attacked her but, if I'm right, this is what's been going on."

Rose put the pieces of paper on the map. Amy and Rob scrutinised her work as she talked them through her reasoning.

"It goes back to mum's death, but to understand how and why we need to start with the day that Sarah gave me those earrings and introduced me to Tony. I have to let both of you know I am not in a good headspace, I want to drink myself to oblivion, but I also want my life back, the one I had ten years ago, before Troy and this stupid illness, the life that I thought I had when I set up the shop, that I was beginning again."

"Before I messed things up for you. Rose, I'm so sorry," said Rob.

"No Rob, I did that to myself, you were a convenient scapegoat, the things I said were wrong, cruel. You supported me through being in prison and afterwards. Maybe that was too much for you, who knows? But we can't blame each other for our downfalls."

Rose pointed to Sarah's name. "The day she gave me those earrings, it was odd, almost as if it was an afterthought. There had been lots of opportunities for her to give them to me beforehand. Meeting Tony that day was a complete fluke, if I hadn't slipped he and I would probably have passed each other without a single word, so when Sarah came after me and gave me the earrings in front of Tony, the fact that I learned later she gave you something too, Amy, it clicked. She was making things for certain students as a signal they might be useful. It was a way of keeping tabs on them, and introducing them to Tony."

"But you said she gave you those earrings as an afterthought." Amy said.

"Yes, and something passed between Tony and Sarah, he wasn't pleased when she told him I was looking for somewhere to rent, yet when I contacted him he turned out to be really helpful, once he realised my back story. That I didn't have a close family and of course my tale about being in prison. It made me useful, vulnerable. You and Alan were in the same league Amy, you have no family and Alan grew up in Thailand. We know Tony was operating some sort of business in Asia, just not what it was. His status as an educator, teaching English as a second language was a great cover. It gave him access to vulnerable students, like Bakti."

"Bakti!" said Rob.

"Yes, remember I said we had got the reason for the murders all wrong, Bakti's murder had nothing to do with you Rob. Bakti was murdered because he had refused to do whatever it was that Tony wanted him to."

"Tony killed him?"

"Well not directly, that's where ... I'm sorry Amy, that's where Alan comes in."

"Alan!"

"Tony is the brains, Alan is the brawn, at least that's what I think. I think it was Alan who attacked Trixie, thinking she was me. We look so different, the only thing we have in common is our height, but Alan hadn't met me before, that's why I was such a shock to him when I arrived at *The King and I*. Tony must have been furious, he hadn't asked him to hurt me, and he had other things on his mind now that he thought the police were onto him and his racket."

"So why did Alan attack Trixie, thinking it was you?"

"Because he was also working for Troy."

"Tony has been running drugs, property, possibly money laundering in Edinburgh for the last goodness knows how many years. He was the invisible man, a respectable member of the community with a lovely wife who had fallen out with his only son. Patrick or Troy, left home when he was eighteen and joined the RAF, back then he was straight as a dye. I'm sure of it. But he had been brought up by a man who was not, perhaps they fell out because Troy found out about his father's so called business, and wanted nothing to do with it. He did however recognise the financial benefits of his father's lifestyle. I believed him when he told me why he retired from service and left the RAF but when Marion was doing some digging she came up with this ..."

Rose showed Rob and Amy her phone. Dishonourable discharge papers. "She sent that over yesterday. I didn't see the relevance until now."

"What was he discharged for?"

"Using other people's identities, his peers in the RAF, it's how he started the financial business. It's really just a Ponzi scheme, I had no idea, even when I worked there it all seemed above board, until of course he had me arrested for fraud. When you came here, Amy and told us you knew Troy as Fraser Hamilton, I thought perhaps Tony and Troy were in competition, that's why I needed to find out if there was a connection. I didn't know then they were father and son. It was when I found the photographs of Tony and Babs and Troy that I began to wonder if they had somehow been working together all this time. We need to find out when Tony and Troy first met again. And the only way I can think to do that is to ask Troy."

"Are you kidding Rose?"

"I don't know how else to find out. I genuinely don't think Babs knows they are in contact. My hypothesis is that after they started working together Troy had no idea his father was renting space to me. When he found out, his determination to destroy me for leaving him bubbled over. I think Troy is behind Sally's murder, Gary's brother's murder, or at least why he was left on my bed and why Alan attacked Trixie. I think Tony is responsible for Bakti, and Dr Reynolds, because he suspected they were selling him out to Snake."

"What about the morphine that was left here?" Rob asked.

"Troy. I think he is out of his mind; that his plans to finish me off, the way he thought prison would, or finding Sally outside the shop, didn't work. Tony had no idea that the man I was referring to when I told him what happened to me was his own son. Tony knew Snake was trying to take over his business. I am pretty sure he didn't suspect it was Troy who killed Sally. Tony killed Dr Reynolds because he suspected he was betraying him.

"So who kidnapped you?"

"I think Troy told Tony some story, so Tony arranged it, there had to have been something in my drink. I was so woozy when I left, I couldn't defend myself. Then of course Tony finds out what Troy had intended to do all along and Tony realised the implications. It set Troy and Tony against each other all over again.

"Sorry Rose, I don't buy it. What implications, both Troy and Tony are murdering people, and Snake? It's too random, too like a bad thriller that's gone wrong, even the author doesn't know who the murderer is."

"You're right."

"Do you think if we talked to Babs it might help? I mean she might know more than we think, maybe a change in Tony's behaviour?"

"She's dying, Rob. Tony disappearing, I don't know what he's told her, she's not involved, I'm sure of it."

"All the more reason to talk to her, support her. The police probably will be asking questions, she might need a friend right now."

"You're right Rob, I'll go and see her tomorrow. Let's take a break, I'll make some food, perhaps you two can go over what I've done, see if you come up with a more rational and realistic outcome?"

Chapter Seventeen

January 7th

Rose didn't recognise the smartly dressed woman putting bags into a Mercedes as she turned into the crescent. She was wearing sunglasses, her long brown curly hair was falling over the shoulders of the baby blue winter coat. Rose walked up the steps of the building where Babs and Tony lived and was about to press the buzzer when she realised where she had seen the distinctive woven shopping basket sitting on the pavement before. It was the one Tony used when he was shopping. She was about to turn around when she felt something sharp digging into her back, a blade penetrated through her leggings and hoodie.

"Push the door open, upstairs now, or I'll use it here," Babs hissed.

Rose hesitated, if she moved in the opposite direction the knife would no doubt pierce her. Rose turned the handle, the lock had been latched and she felt herself being shoved inside the doorway. The blade scratched the surface of her flesh as she stumbled. Babs kicked the door closed and walked step by step behind Rose to the next landing. The door to the flat was open, another bag, a large black suitcase, similar to the one Tony had taken from the travel shop, stood just inside the door.

"You're clearly feeling better then," Rose said as she was forced to walk along the hallway of the apartment. Babs, holding the blade firmly against her, didn't reply.

"Shut up and sit over there," Babs pushed Rose towards one of the high-backed dining chairs. She deftly transferred the position of the blade, it was a small dagger with a snake head handle and an emerald marking the eye.

So much for the lovely Babs who might need a friend, thought Rose, cursing herself for refusing Rob's help and sending him to Glasgow with Amy.

"Put your phone on the table and then your hands behind you," Babs said as she yanked off her scarf, fastened Rose to the chair with it, and left the room. It was hardly an efficient form of bondage, but as Rose wriggled she felt the knot tightening. Babs had clearly done this before. Babs re-appeared in an instant with a roll of silver duct tape.

Rose was about to scream when Troy came into the room.

"Rose, how perfect. It's lovely to see you again my dear." He bent over and brushed her cheek with his lips. The distraction allowed Babs to fasten Rose's feet to the chair.

Rose turned her face and spat at him. "Temper temper, that was always your downfall, Rose. You probably need a drink, I can see you're a bit stressed. Pour her a drink, mother, I can take over here, it's always a pleasure to be close to Rose." He ran his hands over her as if she were an object.

Rose shook her head violently as Troy covered her eyes with tape, she smelled the alcohol under her nose and turned her face away. "Come on now Rose, you know you want it."

She felt two hands cupping her head, pulling it back, another hand pressed her mouth open and held her jaw. The amber liquid began to flood her mouth. She could neither spit it out or hold it, she started coughing, choking on the liquid as it continued to flow. She could feel it running over her face, spilling onto her clothes. She heard Troy laughing as he watched her struggle against the inevitable, pushing the needle into her arm. She had no way out of this. When she came to she was lying on the floor, still attached to the chair. She was gagged, the last thing she remembered was hearing Troy's parting words.

"Let's go mother, no one's going to look for her here, and if they do, we'll be long gone. Goodbye Rose."

Rose had no idea how long she had lain there. The tape covering her eyes meant she had no way of knowing if it was still light or dark. She listened hard for the sound of her phone vibrating or pinging with texts but there was nothing, only the sound of silence. Rob and Amy were in Glasgow with Marion. Surely, they would come to Babs Flat to look for her when they realised she wasn't back, but how would they get in? It could be another twenty-four hours before the police came to look for her. Babs had had her well and truly fooled, Rose revised the solutions she had presented to Rob and Amy yesterday. Of course, it had been Babs and Troy using Tony as a front man.

She had to do something but every time she tried to manoeuvre and wriggle free, she was hampered by the chair. The only thing for it was to try and stand up and use the chair to break a window, hoping she wouldn't fall out of it in the process. The plan eventually worked, her heart was racing when she heard the glass shatter and fall away. The crescent wasn't usually very busy but there would be people coming and going. The air felt cold on her body. Rose stood awkwardly at the window, using the leg of the chair to tap in morse code against the wood hoping someone, anyone, would look up.

"Rose!" It was Rob's voice, she tried to tap louder. She could hear him on his phone calling her, her phone was ringing and vibrating on the table across the other side of the room. She tapped louder. "I'm coming up," he yelled.

She heard the door burst open and Rob's footsteps running towards her. "Oh Rose, what on earth. He removed the tape from her eyes and mouth first."

"What time is it? We have to stop her, tell the DI, I was wrong, it was Babs, it's been Babs and Troy all along."

"What? Here let me get you untied, then you can tell me everything."

"Get my phone, Rob, it's on the table. Call DI Chatterton, he's going to have to listen."

As Rose rubbed her wrists Rob pressed the number for the DI and put the phone on speaker. As soon as he answered Rose gave a quick account of Babs changed appearance, the Mercedes she had been packing bags into and what had happened to her earlier that morning."

"Hold on Rose," They heard the DI giving instructions to locate the Mercedes.

Rose blamed herself that she hadn't taken more notice, even if she hadn't recognised Babs. "Sorry, I should have looked at the numberplate. All I know is the model and that it's white."

"Rose I need to see you, can you come here if I send a car? Do you need medical treatment?"

"No, I'm a mess and I reek of alcohol, but I'm OK. Thanks."

.oOo.

"Trixie has confirmed it was Babs who attacked her," the DI said as Rose sipped on the tea he had brought into the interview room for her. Rose had talked the DI through every detail of her revised hypothesis, and to her surprise he agreed with her. The problem now was evidence. It was past 9 o'clock by the time DI Chatterton requested an officer to drive Rose home.

"Leave evidence gathering to me Rose. You were lucky today; you could have died. I think that was the plan."

"Me too," said Rose.

.oOo.

"Sit," commanded Amy after Rose had taken a shower, and stated she wanted to get back to work, evidence gathering. "I'm making food, if you won't relax, you can read through the notes I took when we met with Marion."

Amy handed her a neatly copied summary of what Marion had said when she and Rob went to Glasgow to see her.

Babs had a long criminal history. She was prosecuted for dealing and fraud in her late teens and served 2 years of a 5 year sentence. She had a son, Stephen who was taken into care. Stephen was two when Babs was sentenced, and she agreed to have him adopted. Babs met Tony soon after she was released, and they had Patrick together. Babs was also dealing again. Perhaps it was because Tony's paycheque as a teacher didn't offer her much in the way of the luxury Babs craved that she started up again. When she was arrested after a car accident, the police found a stash of cocaine under a false panel in the boot of her car and Patrick was taken into care, he was six years old. Tony tried to get custody of Patrick, but the police didn't believe his story that he knew nothing about his wife's involvement as a dealer. It was enough to turn him. His persona as a dutiful husband standing by his woman fooled everyone. But Tony didn't develop the spine Babs needed, he would do so much, but he wasn't going to take the business as far as she needed it to go. Babs was determined to build an empire that supported the lifestyle she had always dreamed of and which would secure a luxurious retirement for her and Tony. Troy turned up eight years ago, just after Rose left him and became a partner in Babs business.

"That's when I think it all started to get more dangerous." said Rose. "Troy came between Tony and his mother, because Troy had the spine Babs needed, he is ruthless. Between them they used Tony to do all the front work, possibly he didn't realise what else was going on behind the scenes, until the murders started. I made it so much more complicated than it was, except for the part about Troy trying to get revenge for me leaving him. I think it was Babs and Troy who killed my mother."

Rob and Amy exchanged glances, neither of them were convinced about this aspect of Rose's conjecture.

"But why on earth would they do that? And why did Babs attack Trixie?" asked Amy. "I hate to say it, but Alan made so much more sense."

"Of course, who would ever think the kindly fey Babs, dying of cancer could ever be responsible for attempted murder."

"And what about the cancer?" said Rob, "I mean she was back and forth to the hospital."

"Do you remember earlier, when the DI let slip about the paramedics and what happened when I went to the hospital? "How clever to have medics involved. I don't know if she was bribing them, or how she did it, but that day she was taken to the hospital by ambulance, it all looked so genuine. It gave her time and an alibi."

"Alibi for what?" Rob asked.

"To see Troy, I'm only guessing, but I think she used the hospital visits as a place to set things up, give instructions. Most people on cancer drugs lose their hair, but Babs never did. I didn't put two and two together until I realised it was her in that brown wig, the same brown wig Trixie had told me she had seen her wearing.

"And Dr Reynolds?"

"He was one of the medics she was bribing. I think Sally found out, perhaps she saw him and Babs together and that's why Babs killed her. It was a senseless and cruel murder. What harm could it have done if Sally had said anything to anyone. No one would believe the word of a user. But I think leaving her dumped outside my shop was Troy's idea. He set it up to remind me of the past, it nearly worked too. Troy probably ran Dr Reynolds over, but when he didn't die, one of the friendly medics finished the job."

"I remember" said Rob.

"That's how Bakti became involved."

"Yes, after he had seen the two men, Troy and Gary's brother put Sally outside the shop. You thought he was terrified about his father visiting, but it was what he knew, if only he hadn't confided in Gary, he would still be alive."

"Tony would not have realised who I was when he rented the shop to me. But of course, Babs and Troy knew all along. I wonder why he waited so long to get his own back, to try and finally finish me off for good."

"So, if he was responsible for the graffiti, why bring attention to the fact that there was a drugs lab upstairs.?"

"No, the graffiti, I think that was Snake. And the wording on the note was pure coincidence. The threat was about drugs and his war with who he thought I was. Remember you told me they thought I was running something. It was a genuine attempt to get me out. I think the graffiti shook Tony and Babs up, it's why Tony was weird that morning when I was talking to the DI and lied about what he knew to Trixie."

"And Trixie, why was she attacked, almost murdered?"

"Because of what she had seen. When Trixie woke up she told the DI she saw Babs that morning. In fact if Rob hadn't got to me at her flat first, the police would have come shortly afterwards, looking for Babs. Trixie remembered waving at Babs going past, about half an hour before she was attacked. She was cleaning the front counter whilst the biscuits were baking. She didn't think anything about seeing Babs with the long brown wig or glasses, because she had seen her wearing them before. Trixie probably assumed Babs was losing her hair due to cancer, and the glasses were to cover how ill she was, after all Trixie hadn't seen her to speak to for ages. It must have given Babs a shock to realise she had been recognised when Trixie waved to her, she probably went home to get what she needed. I think, like me, Trixie was supposed to have died, the way Sally did. I don't know how they messed up the doses, or why Babs and Troy left me in the flat when they could have dumped me somewhere, made it look like I had died, or almost died, from a relapse. I'm sure that's the intention behind why Troy broke into the flat, and why Gary's brother was left on my bed. He thought that I would be charged with attempted murder, that's why they staged the party. Gary's brother was killed because he was greedy, thought he and Snake could take on Babs. Again If I wasn't charged Troy presumed this time it would be enough to make me fall off the wagon, and that would be the end of me."

Amy nodded, remembering the telephone conversation she had heard between Rose and her sponsor.

"So, not Alan then," said Amy. Her eyes were filled with tears. "I feel so bad that I thought he could be a killer."

"I put that in your head Amy, I'm sorry. I mean he's definitely not squeaky clean, but he's not a murderer."

"So why do you think Troy and Babs killed your mother, and how?"

"I suspected Troy for a while, it was why I asked you to go to Bristol Rob, I couldn't understand why my father was so convinced it was me and that my mother's fall was not an accident. I couldn't remember when I lost the charm he showed you. I thought it was after a party where Troy and I had rowed, that would have been about three months before I left him. But then I remembered, it had come off in the bed, I was upset because the chain was broken he was making up to me, he told me he would have the chain fixed, or buy me a new one. Our relationship was really falling apart, I was drinking, he was using and screwing around. When I left he told me I would be sorry, so of course he made sure I was. He took away the one person I was close to. I am sure he thought that if my mother was out of the picture I would go back to him. He couldn't stand how close I was to her, it threatened him and our relationship. Now that I realise he met Babs around that same time, she would have helped him. She would do anything for the son she had lost, and who she realised needed her help to not self-destruct. I had abandoned him, her baby. She was the witness who spoke to my father."

"I still don't get it," said Amy.

"OK, Troy needed me to need him. It's a form of extreme narcissism. He liked it that I had to leave the RAF because of my eyes, it made him feel strong, he wanted to be my knight in shining armour. I wasn't really his type if you look at the women he usually goes for, curvaceous, blonde, feminine. Troy needed someone who he thought would stick with him, grateful for his attention. He gets his kicks out of being in control. I was supposed to become a, a lap dog. It's how he was able to change me from the outside, my appearance, I hated it, and he knew that. He took pleasure in it. but when he realised he couldn't change who I really was he decided to destroy me. When he met his mother again I'm pretty sure she convinced him he was better off without me, but she fed his illness, agreeing with him that I deserved to be punished, the way she had been when he was taken from her. After all she had already lost one baby, losing the second must have been agony for her. I don't know how they killed mum, or when they decided to do it, but me phoning on the day they were at the house was just unfortunate timing. They left the charm there as evidence that I had been there, and then it must have been Babs who spoke to my father, convinced him she had seen me. But of course, I was in Glasgow, and could prove it, although it took a while to convince them you were a reliable alibi Rob. Remember?"

Rob nodded.

"If my father hadn't been so certain about her being killed and that I was responsible, despite my alibi, I would never have thought her death was anything other than an accident, the same conclusion the police and coroner came to. But," Rose shrugged, "there is no evidence for any of this, I don't blame you for doubting me, but I am convinced in my gut, that that's what really happened. The DI said they would look into it, but he wasn't hopeful, after so much time has passed."

"Phew, that's quite a sick scenario Rose. Attachment, bonding, abandonment, there's a psych thesis in what you suggest." Amy said. "But the way you explain it, it does make sense. Your poor father, thinking his own daughter had killed her mother."

"I know, I want to reach out to him, but I'm scared he still won't believe me."

"What about Sarah?" Rob said, "How do they come into this do you think, who beat me up?"

"Ah, well Sarah was a red herring for sure, part of me making things more complicated and seeing things that weren't really there. Rob getting beaten up. That was a coincidence too. Rob was just in the wrong neighbourhood. Babs must have rung rings around Snake. Odd though, her dagger had a snake head handle, with an emerald where the eye would be."

"The sign of a green-eyed monster," said Amy. "Jealously guarding what was hers. There's an Indian myth about such a creature."

Rose yawned, she was exhausted and her body ached from fighting with the chair and her bonds earlier. "Rob, do you feel alright taking the bedroom? I still can't face it."

"It's fine. Although I doubt any of us will get much sleep tonight." But his prediction was wrong and it was almost 9 am before any of them stirred and DI Chatterton called them with some welcome news. Babs and Troy had been arrested. Tony was in custody in Singapore.

.

Chapter Eighteen

Three Months Later

    Rose finished plating the muffins and looked around. The shop had never looked more cosy and welcoming, she thought, thanks to Amy's feng shui, as the dappled sunlight fell across the wall, highlighting the pictures she had hung when it was repainted. How close she had come to losing everything again. Amy too. They had both been surprised when the administrators for the trustees had approached them with an offer to purchase the leases as part of a deal for the new owners. She could hardly bear to think about it . The challenge of recovery after what had happened had made her stronger, more resolved than ever to pursue her dreams. Would her father come, she wondered. Would they finally be able to put the pain that Troy had caused them both to rest? Her thoughts were interrupted by Rob noisily clashing through the door trying to avoid some letters laying on the mat.

    "Smells wonderful Rose," said Rob, handing her the post.

"Thanks to Trixie here, baker superstar."

Trixie beamed. "Och, it feels so guid to be back. I cannae believe the New Year's opening is finally happening on April 1st!"

"Rose, what is it?" Rob said as he watched Rose's face scanning one of the letters he had given her.

"It's Dad, he's not coming," Rose said, as she folded the letter back into the envelope.

"I'm sorry. Do you want to talk about it?"

"Not now, perhaps one day. Today I just want to celebrate, enjoy the day. You, me and Trixie." She put the rest of the post to one side.

"Aye, well now, ye are nae a shite in my book, I suppose we can say we are almost pals," said Trixie, winking at Rob.

"You'd better be pals, I'm not having war going on between my employees, now that Rob is going to organise the marketing and delivery service."

"Aye boss and ..." Her cheeky retort was interrupted by the bell on the door as DI Chatterton came into the shop.

"Good news Rose," he said. "Morning everyone, Trixie, Rob."

"Really?"

"Arrested and charged."

"For my mother?"

"Yes Rose. The procurator fiscal is confident there is enough evidence. Troy and Babs have turned on each other, they did my job for me, trying to negotiate their way out of the other charges. It was a pointless exercise, and Babs solicitor walked, when she ignored her legal advice. On top of what they are already charged with, Babs and

Troy will go away for a very long time. He's wanting the maximum sentence for premediated murder and attempted murder. Tony is on an additional lesser charge for perverting the course of justice."

"Thank you."

"Without your tenacity I doubt we would ever have looked into the charges against you or your mother's death again. But Rose, next time there's a murder, anywhere, please don't try solving it. It nearly cost you your life, and Trixie's."

"Oh don't worry, from now on I'm all about making and baking muffins. Murders I am happy to leave to the police. DI's like you."

"Well, there is one other thing, and that's the fact I'm a DCI now," he beamed broadly.

"Good for you," said Rose. "Now let's send you away with muffins for the station, before this lot eats them all up."

Rose smiled broadly as she looked at the crowd of locals, the lady from the barre studio, the organic grocer, the flower seller and a group of students forming a queue behind him. Muffins on Morrison was back in business.